last

SARAH DAVIS-GOFF

ones

left

alive

TINDER
PRESS

Copyright © 2019 Sarah Davis-Goff

The right of Sarah Davis-Goff to be identified as the Author of
the Work has been asserted by her in accordance with the
Copyright, Designs and Patents Act 1988.

First published in Great Britain in 2019 by Tinder Press
An imprint of HEADLINE PUBLISHING GROUP

2

Cataloguing in Publication Data is available from the British Library

Hardback ISBN 978 1 4722 5520 4
Trade paperback ISBN 978 1 4722 5519 8

Typeset in Sabon by Avon DataSet Ltd, Bidford-on-Avon, Warwickshire

Printed and bound in Great Britain by Clays Ltd, Elcograf S.p.A.

HEADLINE PUBLISHING GROUP
An Hachette UK Company
Carmelite House
50 Victoria Embankment
London EC4Y 0DZ

www.tinderpress.co.uk
www.headline.co.uk
www.hachette.co.uk

'Davis-Goff has crafted a beautiful, lyrical, and
guttural examination of what it takes to love and
survive in a world shaped by loss and violence . . .
truly remarkable and unforgettable'
SARAH SCHMIDT

'Just superb. A visceral dystopian fable of sisterhood
and resilience, animated by fierce, sinewy writing
and a haunting sense of place. Enthralling'
PARAIC O'DONNELL

'This immersive, heart-in-mouth novel is
full of tension . . . filmic, atmospheric, and
reminiscent of *The Walking Dead* if it were set
in apocalyptic Ireland' SINÉAD GLEESON

'*Last Ones Left Alive* gripped me as much by the heart
as it did by the throat' KIRAN MILLWOOD HARGRAVE

'Davis-Goff's writing is crisp and evocative,
her dialogue crackles and sparks, and her gifts
of imagination and narrative verve are present
on every page' DONAL RYAN

'Beautifully written and terrifying, *Last Ones Left Alive* will leave you reeling, not only from its originality and searing vision, but also from the humanity of the relationships portrayed'
KATE HAMER

'Combines the spare poetry of *The Road* with the dizzying pace of *28 Days Later*. A beautiful book, lyrical in its violence, painting in vivid strokes the joy and brutality of the human experience'
JENNIE MELAMED

'What a debut. What a writer. I'm in awe. Sarah Davis-Goff is a true original. I inhaled this book' LIZ NUGENT

'I will be cursing *Last Ones Left Alive* for seriously troubling dreams for weeks to come'
PATRICK GALE

For Mama and Papa

Chapter One

MY TOENAIL HAS BLACKENED AND I'VE TO PULL TO GET it off. You'd feel it, so you would; it's painful enough. I douse my foot in water and I leave the nail by the side of the road and on we go.

This road, this hungry road, eating us up.

We've been walking already for a long time, the three of us together.

Where are the trees and stone walls? Where the abandoned cottages and burnt-out bridge, where the waterfall and the hidden skiff? Where the signposts to lead us back home? I mark them, scraping old metal with jagged rocks, an 'X' that'd mean something only to Maeve and me, one line a little longer than the other for direction. I go over it, making sure I'll remember, while the muscles along my neck and in the small of my back swell and creak with pain. I keep watching all around me.

The blisters I got on my hands from rowing to and from the island fill with fluid, burst, fill again.

When we rest I take leaves of mint from the herb pouch. Mam's herb pouch. My eyes are tired from the glare of the sun. My feet are sore from the too-hot road.

Around us the landscape changes constantly. The road shifts beneath me, twists and slopes, and every time I look up the world presents me with something new and I feel fresh, too. Despite myself, despite everything. The world ended a long time ago but it is still beautiful.

We are moving.

Looking at her lying slumped in the barrow makes my chest feel like it's collapsing in on itself. She is so small – *scrawny* is the word. She never used be small. I look away, and twenty paces later I'm at it again, watching the closed-up face with the sweaty sheen.

We move. We rest again. The dog beside us, the nails on his paws clacking against the road. I can feel the hesitation off him. He's asking me do I know what I'm doing and don't I want to go home.

I do, I tell him. But I can't.

Maeve's lined skin is being burnt by the sun underneath its greyness. I take off my hat and put it on her lightly

2

so most of her face is in shadow. I can pretend that she's asleep. I stop again and rearrange her so that she's facing forwards, facing into whatever's coming at us. She'd feel better that way. I feel better. Maeve wasn't one for looking too often at me anyway unless for a fight.

I've a new pain then, the sun pounding down on one spot at the top of my forehead.

We move. My fear so big, so *palpable*, that it could be an animal walking beside us. I try to make friends with it.

We pause to drink. I shadow-box to show that maybe we're on the road now but I can keep to my training. I nearly feel that I've still some control over what's happening to us, with my fists in the air. I stare at my map, guessing how far we've come from the beach, from home. My eyes and ears are strained long past comfort, waiting to catch the first sign of a skrake bearing down on us.

We get going and we keep going.

I keep an eye on her.

Our road joins a bigger road and that joins a bigger road again, a straight road, and we see more houses and the villages begin to clump together. The road curves upwards and the land thickens into hills. The trees are getting bolder and greener, the landscape transforming every few clicks into shapes and colours I've never seen before. I leave Maeve in the barrow to walk off the road, my back giving out as I straighten, and pull some sticky pine needles to make the tea. It's cooler in the woods, the air smells more the way it does on Slanbeg. Cleaner. I rub the needles in my hands and breathe in deep, letting my eyes stay closed a moment.

Vitamin C, Maeve says in my ear, so clearly that I start, take in a sharp breath. I go quickly back to the road.

Her body is prone in the barrow, her lips closed into a disapproving line.

Every now and then there'll be a tree growing right up in the middle of the road and I have to unpack the barrow and carry everything round. Food, blankets, the chickens squawking. I try not to breathe when I lift Maeve. I try not to feel her bones.

Progress is slow, slower even than I thought it would be. Danger lies down to watch me and pant in the shade of a stone wall standing all on its own. He waits till I've slogged past him and then he gets up and shakes himself and lollops along again.

It's viciously hot till the sun starts to sink, then suddenly it's cold. The clouds come down on us, obstinate and dour.

When the storm comes it lights up the darkening sky with violent intensity. I stop and lift my head to watch, my hands in the small of my back to stretch it out. It feels dangerous, pausing, but I linger and even let my stinging eyes close, and when it starts raining I take the hand-wraps off and hold my palms up and offer them to the deluge.

We're moving east, striking out opposite to home, but sometimes the road takes us north or south or even west again for a while. I don't know are we going along the path we should at all.

I look to Maeve and ask her again which way. She has nothing to say to me.

I think about food; I think about Mam's old way of saying it: *The hunger is on me.* That's it. I've lost condition, and the dog was skinny enough starting out. The chickens are subdued in their makeshift crate. Around me the sky crackles and combusts.

I do nothing but walk, and we get nowhere. Sometimes we pass road signs that are still legible: Doolin, Lisdoonvarna. I tick them off the tattered map. I'm not watching out around me enough, I know that without Maeve telling me, and so after every fifty steps I take one careful look in all four directions. It's good to stretch out my neck, to take in the landscape, a balm for my eyes still. Then I'm back watching the top of her head and I begin the count again.

I make lists as I push, of all the things I'm afraid of. Going back to the island. Never going back. Skrake. People, especially men.

While we walk, and then when I can walk no more, I try to get my brain to linger over home. In case I haven't another chance at it, I try to think of Mam. Her smell, like warm herbs. She used to sing. I hum to myself, trying to remember a tune. The noise that comes out of me sounds nothing like her songs and I should be keeping quiet. I don't want to be adding to the noise my feet are making on the road, the roll of the barrow's wheel, the racket of me pushing and pulling through trees and over debris. Skrake are attracted to noise. Noise and fire and movement. Their vision is good and their smell is exceptional, and they're afraid of nothing. And they've a taste for us, so they do.

I wonder instead what Mam'd be at now, if she were me. She wouldn't have stayed on the island either. Mam would be proud of me.

Wouldn't she, Maeve?

My throat is dry and all I want is to stop and drink and then collapse and lie still for a long time, days and nights. We press on. Danger lags so far behind, his lithe black and white coat a dark smudge against the horizon. I wonder if he'll bother catch up at all.

It is the first day of our walk.

Chapter Two

I HAD A CHILDHOOD AND IT WAS HAPPY, AND THE FACT THAT my mother and Maeve were able to do that for me while the country was ate around us says probably everything anyone needs to know about them.

The sun rises on Slanbeg and us with it. I hear the soft noises of the hens, the rooster making a racket no matter what the hour. Stretching in the bed while Mam cooks eggs downstairs. The smells and the sounds and the feeling of warmth even in the winter while the panes of glass had frost the whole way across and the ice storms went on for days.

Farming in the heat. We wear hats with brims against the sun. Mine is too big and keeps falling down over my ears. The lazy sound of a bumblebee and over that, singing. The sun warm on my shoulders, the smell of wholesome things growing, of grass and peas and ripening tomatoes. Maeve passes me with her bucket full of weeds and puts her rough hand on the back of my neck for a moment and I feel like my chest could heave full open, spilling red happiness on the hot thirsty earth.

One happy memory is a million when you're growing up, one summer afternoon a decade of them. How many days spent by the sea, making dams and collecting shells and seaweed. Lying on a rug in the warmth with an arm thrown over my eyes against the sun, smelling the salt on my skin and digging my toes into the sand. Straying over to watch the creatures in rock pools, only to look up with a question and see Mam and Maeve talking quietly together, stopping to kiss, fingers touching.

Or later, watching them spar, showing me the holds and pressure points and the right curve in a hit. Sitting in the wild grass watching, the chickens bawking and eyeing me to see if I'll find a slug for them.

The water nearly warm in the big plastic basin she put before the fire. Winter again, the rain raging against the windows, and I nearly feel sorry for it being so cold and lonely and wanting to get in. There's a towel warming for me on a rack before the hearth and I know when I get out of the dirty water in a minute she'll wrap it around me, from ears to feet. She'll tell me I'll be as snug as a bug.

Making up stories for me once I'm in my night-clothes and we've finished stretches. Maeve says not to be filling that child's head with rubbish, the half-laugh that used be in her, the light the both of them gave out.

The point being in any case that I had a home and I was loved and that was really fucking obvious even if everything else was a mystery.

Chapter Three

STAY CLEAR OF TALL BUILDINGS. MAEVE'S ADVICE. THERE IS no way round that I can see, not unless we go back, unless I unload and load up the barrow all those times again to get over the trees and gaps and cracks. Going back never seems the right thing to me.

I shade my eyes against the sun and look on ahead of us at the town, trying to see might anything fall down on top of us.

'Is it the right way?' I ask Maeve, and I ask it out loud, my voice a tremble, in case she can hear me. I'm nearly afraid she'll answer, and then when she doesn't I feel a swell of pure rage.

We'll go through. If these were going to fall they'd have

fallen already, they would. And I want to look, anyway; I want to see a bit of the lives that were led in the towns here in Ireland.

We go on straight so and the buildings get bigger the way the trees did before till we're surrounded by them. We go slow and we go quiet, I'm awake now and looking around and my stomach is in my throat. Glass crunches beneath us. I see shadows and reflections.

I see a dark shape out of the corner of my eye and a half-turn, a breath, is all I manage before it is on top of me. The barrow goes sprawling and the back of my head is smacked into the road. One hand comes up reflexively towards my belt but the other is pinned behind my back as I fall.

I can do nothing at all. I can't think or breathe or blink or move. I've no answer for this thing on me.

Move!

Maeve. It's the edge in her voice in my head that gets me going.

I try to push myself up and can't, but get a breath in at least. The smell of rotten meat hits me and I hear, nearly feel, teeth clacking together, trying to snatch a mouthful off out of me. I throw an elbow up and thrust. It's flimsy and I go again, harder. The weight on me shifts a little. I smash, my elbow bruising, and again, and then both hands are free, and the weight lifts enough to let me get up as far as

11

my knees. Danger is barking hoarsely. It's everywhere, snapping its teeth furiously, and it's the most I can do to push the head away with both hands. The teeth are just a whisker off my ear. I can feel the skin and hair shift beneath my palms, its flesh coming away from rotting sinew and muscle and bone. Its dead breath is overwhelming. I fall backwards and the skrake doesn't break for a second before it comes at me again fast, so *fast*, but I get a foot under it and pitch hard upwards as I land (*Sacrifice throw*, Maeve says. *Good*), and with a desperate thrust I get it most of the way over my head.

I get up to my feet and get back to put more space between us and I crouch low and ready. I've an anger on me now that I have my breath, now that I'm not so panicked. I feel it all the way up from my toes. My fingers go to my belt and I let fly.

My hands are shaking with the fright but the knife gets into the skrake's chest and I feel like I'm going to win: I feel like I'm getting something back, I'm clawing something away from the dread I've in me. I can see it gather itself together for another attack, and without looking for it my second knife is in my hand. I back up a few steps more as it reaches for me, aim for the skull and I throw. The knife glances off.

Danger has the skrake's lower leg in his mouth. I think I shout while I pick another knife, toss, catch and throw again, aiming again for the head, and I'm wondering stupidly if I can even pierce a skull from this distance, and all my life bloody training and really I have no idea, I know *nothing*. The head moves to the left as Danger pulls harder on its leg and the knife glances off again.

I take a breath through my nose. I try to calm down. I reposition myself with one knee beneath me on the ground and one knee forwards. The skrake is going to shake off Danger or he'll get hurt, and I move my hand to my knife-belt again, bring it up, let fly. This one catches it full force in the throat but the skrake doesn't stop and I get my hands out nearly as it lands on me: I roll sideways, get to my feet and crouch low, trying to gather myself before it comes at me again.

Syrupy black blood is oozing from its injuries but the skrake keeps coming. It grabs my hair and an arm, whatever is in reach, and pulls me apart while its teeth go for my head. I arch my back, try to get a knee between us, and loose a hand so I can get hold of the knife still lodged in its neck. I pull it out and the skrake gives a deep gurgling noise: blood throbs out much faster now, drenching my clothes. I stick the knife in again and feel it weakening at last. I don't stop. The knife meets soft flesh and gritty flesh and bone, and when I pull it out the blood spurts on to me and it's all I can do to keep my face out of the flow. I worry about the sores on my hands.

I push it off me, feeling the shakiness, the weakness in my arms. I don't let myself lie there even for an instant. I move.

I'm on my feet, in a guard position, watching.

I breathe, in and out.

Blood – dark, viscous, clinging – is everywhere. I do my best to wipe it from my face. Out of the corner of my eye I see the skrake incredibly – predictably – making to get up. Ruined eyes roll in decayed sockets and its proboscis, pink smeared with black, throbs in the dark cave of its mouth.

The fear is gone and I feel revulsion and then anger. I use it: I rush at the skrake, low and fast. I gather its legs and keep pushing till it's on its back and I land on it hard as I can, pinning with my knees. I reach for my ankle-knife and go for the eyes and the mouth.

It seems like a long time again till the skrake goes still but in the end it gives way.

It's small, I can see now.

It was just a child, half the size of a full-grown one. Half the strength. I try not to look too hard, but at the same time I don't take my eyes off it. The body isn't far gone. There's jeans, tied with a belt that somehow still hangs on to that skinny waist. It has a jumper, shoes on it still. One lace tied and the other trailing and filthy.

I lie still again until my breathing is more normal and then I get up and I tie the lace.

14

Maeve lies in the barrow, just the same, dustier maybe from being inside the buildings. I nearly thought something would stir her and she'd be up.

We go on, quick and quiet, just like I've been trained, and soon we're through the town and back out on to the lonely roads and I push hard.

I want to put distance between us and the corpse before the light starts to go. I'd half thought, I'm only after realising now, that maybe I'd get all the way east without seeing any skrake at all.

I think again about turning round and going back and doing the thing I'm supposed to do instead of striking out this way. My mind does the same sums and comes to the same conclusions, though, and on I keep.

You'd nearly expect skrake to be outlined in red or something the way I was told about them. With pictures Maeve had drawn, badly, targets for knife-practice, with long descriptions, repeated till I knew them by heart. They'd been half mythic, half nonsense. But they're just grey and ordinary, kind of, part of the background, human-shaped and unobvious. Till they're going for your throat.

When the afternoon's storm comes, I put the tarp lightly over the barrow and we keep walking. I turn my face up to the sky and wipe it with a cleanish bit of my shirt. Danger

15

walks almost on top of my heels with his tail between his legs.

I move so fast now my feet nearly trip over themselves. My fingers grip the handles of the barrow till they cramp and I have to shake them loose, but I hardly get them unclamped before I pick it up again and get us on our way.

I am spooked is what I am. My eyes rove around the countryside, looking for movement. I cannot stop thinking about the way the skrake felt beneath my fingers. So dead. Twice killed.

'Maeve. MAEVE.' I say it over the weather. She says nothing back.

'I am spooked,' I say to her then, but quietly. I want to own up to it.

How often are skrake alone?

I push the barrow as if we are being chased. I imagine I see them everywhere, in bits of plastic blowing in the winds and when bushes sway and when we turn a corner in the road. Danger skitters along, tail still low, stopping to look back at me and the road, then me again. *Come on*, he is saying. *Quick*.

We stop eventually, right by the road. I'm so dead on my feet that suddenly to go even a little further seems impossible. The shelter must once have been a shop. There's a massive metal roof outside covering rusty, cowering machines. One side of the building is smashed clear away like a giant fist took a swipe at it.

I'd stay clear of tall buildings but it's stop here or stay out of the rain so I take the risk of it. There's broken glass everywhere inside and pushed-over shelving units. There's papers and I gather them up, and dust and more glass. On the papers, and on some of the bottles I see now is that same drawing you see everywhere with the cup and the snake.

I get Maeve out of the barrow and on to the blankets I've laid out for her and listen hard in the perfect quiet. I pour some water into her mouth, just a trickle. I can't be sure that any goes down her throat.

In the near-dark, I walk around the shop, touching things, trying to read. Danger walks nearly on top of me, wanting to be close, and I'm glad of him though he should stay and watch for Maeve. The shelves are long empty, matted with dust, broken. I can see the trail of fingers, fingers that were here long before mine, trailing the dust that had already gathered on these empty shelves, finding nothing. A print, perfect nearly, on top of a counter. I put my own sore hand in it and try to imagine another life. I can see footprints, too, in the fading light, very old ones with shoes and then two newer sets, bare, and then mine and Danger's.

When I open the chicken crate they show no interest in leaving, only blink slowly at me. I look at Maeve, her crumpled form wrapped in the damp tarp on the ground. I don't kill one, in the end, only because I can't bear one more dead thing around me.

Chapter Four

IF YOU'D GO INSIDE THEM OTHER HOUSES ON SLANBEG AND
I always did, I was always looking for something, you'd
see into lives from long ago.

These are wrecked on the inside as well as the outside.
Mam let me at it OK but Maeve didn't like me going in,
she said we'd learned all we could already from ghosts,
and I wasn't to go digging around in lives not belonging
to me. Mam and Maeve had been in the houses as well,
though, I could see their prints, and that took the shine off
Maeve's argument.

They've got away with a lot, these houses. They've
their four walls standing and the roofs, too, for the most
part. I'd get in where I could and there was somewhere

that was easy on all of them, I'd know it by heart. So I'd slip through the window that was broken or never had any glass or even sometimes just plain through the front door.

Everything is covered in dust and dirt, but you can nearly see, you can guess at the lives that went on in them walls. All the presses with electrical things inside them that haven't moved, and the chairs that were last sat on by live people in families. So many things still neat after all this age. Upstairs are the beds, same as ours, and books and papers I'd pilfer, and the other stuff now that seems only sadder the more I look at it or think on it. The empty beds. The little socks, no bigger than my palm. Your heart would break for them, so it would.

There's a feeling in some of the houses that you're *near* the families, that they're only outside the back and will come in again for their tea in a moment. They're so present, these dead people, the dead kids my own age and the littler ones.

The desperate came looking, so they did. People wanting shelter from the skrake, and then from the hunger, trying to get into the houses here, to take whatever these people had. You see it around the island – the smashed windows, remnants of small, desperate battles, the dusted bones. All gone a long time ago now, whether by hunger or sickness or the hands of each other. No skrake got this far, Mam and Maeve told me, and that is a warning as well – there's warnings all around us on this island about monsters that aren't skrake. If there were any of them left when I was a child, Mammy and Maeve would have made sure they were no danger to us anyway.

On the outside ours is as wrecked as the others, or worse, and boards on the windows, but mostly so that you can't see that behind them the glass is in one piece still.

The inside of ours is a living house. Mam and Maeve stole and pilfered and looted, if you can do those things to the dead and undead and never born, which I'd argue you can't, until they had ours looking the way they wanted it. Like a home. You wouldn't know we were in a ghost-house in a ghost-estate and a ghost-country, the way I was reared in that house.

I'd everything I needed, nearly, food and clean water and baths and beds and there were books I was allowed and others I was not. We'd comfort, rugs and blankets, and plants brought inside to save them from the winter. We'd the stories Mam would tell about heroes, making me want to be brave, stories about Gráinne the pirate queen, and the Morrígan and Brigid and Maeve, who I confused with our Maeve.

In a painting on our wall there's a man who might be dead or might just be sleeping, and there's just a little bit of blue in the grey of the bleak clouds. You can see mountains, and the man might be looking at them, if he isn't dead. My mother loved this picture. I'm named Orpen, even, after the painter.

There's other pictures – a naked man, and a woman asleep in an orange dress with a calm sea – but this one with mountains is the best; it's the one that looks most *likely* to me. I wonder was the artist some kind of prophet that he could see the trouble we'd be getting into, making a picture like this so long ago when the world was whole. That's what painters were, maybe.

I looked a long time at these pictures growing up, trying to figure them out, and I did in the end. It's a warning, not to be caught out on your own, not to get left on your own, ever, not if you can help it. It made sense to me then when I realised that this was the problem I had here on the island, this was the cold space I felt within me.

There was evidence of it all around us, of people living together in families and groups. There're no houses off on their own on this island, they're together. People are meant to be together and I knew that and the painter knew that, but here we were, on our own. Especially me.

I kept looking, I looked all around the island with a hunger on me to know more about how it was when the world was whole, I read everything. In the houses, in old papers, there was more of it, signs of people all gathered up. I went further all the time, out to places I wasn't meant

22

to go on my own and I ate up the pictures, of businesses and towns and cities and countries. I kept going till I first read that word 'banshee' and that was only the start so it was.

Chapter Five

B Y THE TIME THE SUN COMES UP WE'RE ON THE ROAD.
I heave us up bad hills and hold the barrow tight
when we come down the other side. Rolling green and
dazzling blue every direction, so lush, so *verdant*, I want to
open my mouth and eat it in slices. We see: a church made
of stone, its crosses fallen away but three grey walls
standing, and a tree growing up through a raised platform
on the eastern side; a place where the ground is flat and the
grass, for no reason I can see, growing only in inches, a
perfect circle; in a hollow of land a lake but out of the
water spike the tallest parts of buildings, chimneys and the
tops of towers and a spire. Everywhere there is life, birds
and biting insects, rats near water and small animals that'll

rush out of the overgrowth ahead of our steps making my heart leap into my mouth and my hand toward my knife a half-dozen times a day.

I let my eyes go where they want to as long as my feet are moving us forwards.

Danger is still limping but he's no worse than yesterday anyway. He's not used to seeing so many cars and he stops to inspect them, sniffing carefully, weeing everywhere but on the flat, crusted wheels especially. Then he comes back to me looking for the water I'm breaking my back carrying.

Later in the day, when the sun is a few hand-spans up into the sky, I've to put down the barrow and drag him away from something: a dusty pile of bones with its leash caught in a car window. I peer inside through the grimy windows at the leathered shapes. So close to each other but unable to move: surrounded by skrake, terrified, starving or dying of thirst or heat. Stinking of shit. Women, children. Men. They'd no good choices, these people; we've that in common.

I'm more frightened today and more steely too. There will be more skrake and it's just a matter of when and how, and if I can beat them. I strain my ears and I touch my knives and I keep my wits about me.

We move, aiming east.

Around us Ireland only becomes more beautiful and more alien. I can smell the rich dark earth.

Just a few more days, I tell myself. I'll get more out of her yet, and being on the road is still better than being on that fucking island.

I keep pushing. I want to get as far as Athlone by the time it rains, and when the road turns north and the sun's out of my eyes I take it as a little victory and the three of us stop and rest in the shade of some greenery. I watch the low sprawling town awhile from here and swat away bugs, and I drink and mooch around in the barrow for something to eat. I mean to share a tin of something – the label long gone off it – with Danger, but I'm so hungry it's gone before I know where I am. Instead he gets the last of the cooked potatoes, which are squashed and starting to smell bad. He's them ate in three heartbeats and then he sits down to fart and stare dolefully at me for more.

I'd set the chicken crate on the road and let open their little door, and after a few moments two of them come out and bawk and blink in the sunlight. They drink down their water and peck. I can feel Danger beside me wanting to go for them but he knows he's not allowed. He thumps his tail on the ground in embarrassment.

I doze. If a skrake comes at me now I'll be in trouble, but isn't it always the way?

My feet, used as they are to walking, feel pinched and bald in my shoes. I know I should take them off and air

them but I can't face it, and going barefoot feels dangerous now. Not being able to move quickly could be death.
How right Maeve was, I think. My eyeballs are tired
with trying to take in the stern landscape against the glare
of the sun and the unyielding blue of the sky. They have
me caught between them, like pincers, and together they
squeeze.

I breathe deep against the relentless wind and feel that
my life has begun.

In the end we don't get as far as Athlone but we do OK
and I'm happy enough to get off the road and find somewhere on the outskirts of the big town. The countryside is
so much greener than I'd imagined. It's all the rain. The
ground is flat again but the earth is so thronged with
growth that I can only sometimes see the horizon. There's
trees growing right up through the smaller road we're on,
casting a green shadowy light over us, protecting us from
the lurid sun. We've to stop often to unpack or hack a way
through them and it's tough going now and only getting
harder. I look over at Maeve in case she's anything to say
to me about this but she doesn't and my mind wanders
while we work.

Sweating, being stung by a hundred hungry bugs, I slash
our way forwards till, suddenly, we're at a clearing, and it's
beautiful. The earth here is covered in soft grass, and under
the largest trees grow small white flowers. Snowdrops.

There are none on the island but my mother brought me back some once and showed me how to dry them between the pages of a book. I thought it was stupid at the time, but I know now how it must have been, to see beauty like this, to need to try and share it.

'Maeve, look,' I whisper.

Low, one-storey buildings, old-looking and made of brick; doorless, roofless, glassless. Ash trees find shelter behind the walls and grow up through chimneys, thrusting fresh green leaves through caving holes in the roof. Then more greenery, and a lone cottage standing just off the small road I've found. The front windows are gone, but otherwise it looks neat, almost intact.

Good shelter. Maeve'd approve of me doing things properly this time instead of hanging around getting us all caught out in the storm and catching our deaths with it. I put the barrow aside quietly and draw a knife.

Danger hops along through the wild grass with me. It takes a while for my eyes to adjust to the gloom. I move carefully, expecting horrors round every corner, but the little house has been cleaned out. Whatever could be ate went first, and then whatever could be burnt.

In the best-preserved room I find what I'm looking for, but there're only a few books left on the broken-down shelves and they're soggy from the roof leaking on them. I go through them hungrily but the pages come away in my hands and the ink has run. I try to imagine the hands that held them last.

I should go back out to the barrow but the shadows inside the cottage are cool and it feels so good to have my back straightened out, to be walking unencumbered. I go into another, darker room towards the back of the house, a bedroom. The two windows and what's left of the ceiling are overgrown with ash, moss and cobwebs. The light in the room is musty and yellowish. There's a good inch of dust underfoot and the room smells sad but not evil. It'd be all right to defend, some part of my brain is thinking, for a while, if you had to, but mostly I'm staring at the iron bedstead in the middle of the room. It has the remains of a bedspread on it. There are blotches of faded colour, a brown that might have been bright red once, and I can't tell if it's part of some old pattern, or whether it is something else.

There are shapes under the covers. I feel very still and very heavy, but my feet are moving towards the bed and my hand is reaching out to the coverlet.

There is a noise behind me.

'Orpen.'

I turn, knowing in my heart that I'm only imagining her voice again, she's such a part of me.

But it is her.

It's Maeve.

She stands in the doorway, using it for support, to help hold her up. Her eyes are on me, glassy and bright.

'Maeve,' I breathe, and my throat feels like someone has a hand around it.

Her face is still pale, her lips drawn back over her teeth. There is a smell like rotten vegetables clumped together. It's just like the last time.

'Orpen,' she says again, so sweetly, so invitingly. She has never said my name like that before; she always said it like she'd stones in her mouth. Mam was the sweet one to me.

Maeve reaches an arm out towards me.

Tears topple down my face, my nose is running.

My feet won't budge. I'm more frightened now than I was with the skrake.

'*Orpen.*'

I take a step back.

'Come here.'

'Maeve,' I say, and try to make it stronger and do the thing I've been waiting to do since I put her in that barrow. 'Maeve, where's Phoenix City?'

She says nothing back, only coughs, and then her shoulder gives a kind of twitch and then she looks at me again.

'Where's the city?' I say, louder and bolder in this little space where I'll probably die now, where Maeve will kill me at last.

'Come here,' she says, no fake sweetness in it now and I nearly do, I'm so used to obeying her, but for the smell off her, the smell of death. 'It's to the east,' she says when I don't move. 'Come here and I'll tell you . . . come here, it's on your map . . .'

Maeve reaches for me again, brushes my forearm before I move back another step. Her nails are long, the edges frayed and broken. I'll go no further towards her but I'm battling my revulsion, my *horror*, as I try to hold my ground.

'Come here, you—' Maeve lunges for me but misses, tries to hang on to the doorway but slips, one foot flailing out in front of her. She lands hard on the ground.

The backs of my legs are pressed against the bed but Maeve is crawling towards me now, her face turned up towards me, her lips peeled back in a snarl.

I climb up on the bed and even in my fright feel my shoe do something new and biting to my left foot.

'Where are we, what have you done, you *bitch*?' Maeve is screaming.

And I scream back, I bawl, 'Where is it, Maeve, where is the city?'

She reaches for me and I take another half-step back and I'm cornered; there's nowhere else for me to go. Her thin lips are drawn back from her greying teeth, her skin seems nearly to be coming away off her. She is monstrous and I am half sobbing, half moaning. My hand goes to my knife-belt.

She goes sweet then again, suddenly wheedling, as her strength gives out.

'I'm sorry, I'm so sorry, forgive me. Come here, come here to me, come here to your Maeve.' Her voice is getting weaker and she's having trouble lifting her head off the ground. 'Come . . .' Her voice is full of muck and dust. She twitches, then lies still.

I fall to my knees on the bed and wrap my arms around my face and I cry.

Chapter Six

I'M SIX AND WILL BE SEVEN. SEVEN IS BIG. SEVEN MEANS I'LL be out of being a child and into being a girl and aiming to be a woman. I'm to put away the stories about the monsters that are not real and to hear about the others. They've got worse as I got older; heroes are caught, turned, burnt, throttled, they die of hunger and cold. Children same as me. Maeve listens approvingly. Mam mops up my tears and comes to me if I scream at night but she doesn't stop telling them.

They're easier to talk about in the day; we are gardening when I tell the two of them I'd nightmares again, about monsters.

'Ghosts and giants are just stories,' Maeve says, not stopping what she's doing to look at me.

'But skrake are real?'

'Real enough to kill you dead,' Maeve says. She has shown me her scars: her ear gone clean from her head, the long red and white welts on her back.

'But there're none on the island,' Mam reminds me. She stands and stretches out her back, putting one hand against the sun.

Home always feels safe; death seems so far away when Slanbeg is full of life, when everything grows so fast and desperate, when the weeds need to be attended constantly. I look away from Mam and let my fingers back into the cool earth.

'How many people are there in the world?' It's questions like these I've been thinking about more and more, and it's easier to talk when we're all busy with our hands in the muck and feeling easy with each other.

Nobody says anything.

'Where did everyone go?'

'Skrake got 'em,' Maeve says, almost with satisfaction, and I feel myself get a little colder even in the hotness of the day.

Mam sighs. 'The skrake, love, everyone was trying to get away from them.'

'That and the hunger,' Maeve says. 'Men can do terrible things, Orpen. Don't forget that.'

This is new.

'Men?'

Maeve tips her head. 'Men made the skrake, long ago.'

'By accident,' Mam puts in, and Maeve nods again.

'They did terrible things then and they do terrible things now.'

'How do you know?'

'Know what, little warrior?' says Mam.

'That men made the skrake and that men are still doing terrible things.'

Mam and Maeve glance at each other and neither one answers so I go back to the thing I want to know most.

'How many people are left?'

'Whisht, child, do your weeding now.'

Time passes and I'm thinking about something else completely when Mam says, 'We don't know, Orpen. We don't know how many people are left. We're the only ones on the island, anyway, and we know there are some people left in Ireland, but nobody knows about anywhere else.'

'We don't know that,' Maeve says. 'We don't know there's anyone left on the mainland.'

'But we should look,' I tell them, and my voice sounds young in my own ears even.

Mam and Maeve look at each other and then Maeve says, 'Good idea, Orpen. Muireann and me will take you to the mainland and we'll introduce you to some nice skrake.'

I've nothing to say back to her and I know she's only trying to make me afraid, and I am, and I stay quiet.

Chapter Seven

WE WALK. ALTHOUGH MAEVE FACES FORWARDS IN THE barrow, I know that if I put the barrow down to look I'll see her twitch and chew. Sooner or later she'll come for me again.

We move. I hardly sleep. We come across no one, neither sight nor sound. Maybe Maeve was right and there's only ghouls and ghasts left in this land.

Her feet and hands are bound and when we stop to rest now I tether her to something solid. To the north, a ruin, a castle, swallowed nearly completely now back into the earth, vines of creeper wood and reaching up through the grass like grasping fingers.

I've no time for beauty now.

Maeve drinks however much water I give her: sometimes her eyes are glazed and sometimes she stares at me closely, suspiciously. I ask her again about Phoenix City; she doesn't answer me. Sometimes she says a word, but the word is not hers. She calls me 'darling' and I feel that she's already gone.

Because I am so frightened, because I cannot sleep, we make good progress. I come off the main road before the rains to find shelter, but the town we're nearest to has nothing for us but the long-ago remains of four large corpses and one small one, tied to trees. All we can make out now is clothes and bones. I try not to look close but the sun catches off a piece of metal, a necklace that still rests around a neck, and before my stupid mind can catch up with itself I'm thinking about who'd have put it there. Danger sniffs them and I don't have the energy to get him to stop.

I am limping.

We move. I check my map and we pass signs for Portlaoise and to Kildare. I check the towns small and big for the words 'Phoenix City', but it's not there, never mind what Maeve says. We're past the halfway mark between east and west, well past it, and we keep on going.

I have spent so long now bent over my burden that my back might never straighten again. Still and all, we keep going.

* * *

I'm singing to myself under my breath in a sort of half-daze of an afternoon when I realise there is something singing with me.

The wheelbarrow is squeaking. I'm not sure how long it makes the noise before I hear it, and how long then till I understand what a danger it is. Any noise will mean skrake might hear us, and then *our* being skrake. Which is no good, so it's not.

'That's no good,' I whisper to Maeve.

The dog eyes me warily and gives a low whine.

I stop and crouch, the muscles along my back stretching and groaning as I kneel and try to wrestle my brain into thinking. I blink hard, feeling dazzled by the sun. It's the coupling for the wheel: a washer is gone rusty and stiff. I did not think to bring tools or parts or even oil with me. I sit down in the middle of the road and put my face in my hands and when I've finished doing that I get up again. The rain isn't far off so I backtrack to the exit only half a klick behind us and we strike out for a town.

I'd glimpsed the roofs of houses in the far-off from the road whenever there were gaps in the trees and now I see them up close. I push slowly, feeling as if I'm being watched from every broken window. The whole fucking country is haunted, I'm after learning, not just our little island.

With every second step the wheel squeaks and we're so

exposed I'm wondering should I have stayed on the road, stupid skrake-attracting shitter of a barrow and all.

'Maeve. Should we've stayed going?' I wipe a grimy hand through my hair. 'Maeve?'

Maeve says nothing.

Up ahead, though, I can see the road widening and there are buildings against the road with yawning broken squares at their fronts. The squeak is only getting louder and I try to lean to the right and then to the left to see can I get it to whisht, racking my brains for what I could use as a lubricant that'd last me another day.

'Cunt of a yoke,' I hiss to the barrow.

The squeaking is so loud in my ears half of Ireland must be able to hear it, if there's anyone left.

There're more signs at the side of the road, big ones for Dublin and other places. They've writing on them, and though I can recognise the letters I can't read the words, and the bits I can read make no sense to me, except for the ones you see everywhere, the ones saying 'She Has Come' and 'Run', and then circles and triangles and arrows and the like. One, a big metal sheet that had been painted blue once, has half fallen from its place and I'm able to wheel the barrow round the back of it so it's mostly hidden. I tell Maeve to hang on tight and then Danger gets up from his panting in the shadows to come with me.

'Mind her,' I tell him. 'Danger? Sit.'

He sits down again, looking grateful.

I check my knives and go on alone towards the town. The quiet is unearthly now I don't have that squeaking in my ears. My breath is loud in the silence. The slap of my feet against cracked road and root and plant could be the rhythm of the whole world.

There's plastic, broken glass, empty and squashed tin cans, and I pick my way carefully along, looking over my shoulder for skrake, towards where I hid Maeve, every few moments. It takes my eyes a long time to adjust to the gloom of the inside of the first shop I reach and I don't go inside but rest for a minute, my eyes closed, my hand against the empty window frame. I am light-headed. I do not know when last I ate.

Oil.

I'm not going to find oil, not in this shop, maybe not anywhere. I wriggle my toes and wonder how long a little blood might keep the barrow wheel slick.

I'm getting dizzily to my feet when it runs past me, a distance away.

A shape, dark and large, going past me at a run.

It's gone before I've time to register what it is but I can hear it, moving north past the lines of shops, and it disappears into the shrubs just as I clamber back out on to the street. A skrake? I don't have the fear I'd have if I'd seen a skrake. It was bigger, running straighter, making more noise. My knife is in my hand and I follow, unthinking, head spinning, belly rumbling. My feet bounce off the road; the branches and glass and scattered rubbish can't hurt me. I am hungry is all. That's why it's hard to get up and my head is swimming.

I push quietly through the growth northwards after whatever animal I glimpsed. I won't go far, I think, I'll only take a minute. The greenery is so much thicker here. What little is left of the road is a different colour entirely from the bluish-purple of the road to the city. Like it's been swallowed up and spat back out and is barely a path, a rough line, like a finger drawn across dry dirt. It smells wetter down here off the main road and the trees have a lushness, a freshness and coolness to them, and I feel the fug and heat in my head start to ease off me.

I breathe deep, in and out, and press on further.

The land beneath my feet swells upwards and to the left, and there's a feeling about heading westward that seems such a relief – as if I have been moving against a strong current for these last days and now I've turned and let it take me towards home.

I go on a ways, knowing I should turn back: I haven't seen or heard the animal I saw, even if I did see something, and Maeve is alone. I think of turning round and picking up the barrow again and I can't, so just for a while longer I keep climbing. Breathing deeply, moving fast, feeling the air in my lungs good and fresh and new. There's a ridge ahead of me, off the track to the left, and I think I'll go and climb that and have a short little rest and I'll be on my way. Maybe I'll even see something from the top, see the place I'm looking for or a road to it, leading east.

I hear it before I see it. Something moving through the trees. Fast, large, coming nearer – along the path. I realise it's animals that have kept it a path all these years, through this forest once the old road crumbled away. Animals or skrake or maybe both. I feel calm; I look about me as the noises get louder and up at the tree above me, and I jump to grab on to a branch and I pull myself up. I climb and then stop to listen.

It bursts out of the undergrowth to my right and I'm safe enough up away out of it, but still and all I jump half out my skin. It's a monster, four-legged and massive, with antlers wide as its body and nearly as long, and bloody with flesh living and dead hanging off them. My knife goes to my belt but the animal is so big it'd be like trying to bring down a skrake with a needle. A deer, nearly, but massive.

It shakes itself out into the clearing and then stops and I stay still and hold my breath and will it not to see me.

The incongruity of it. What a ridiculous thing to be alive, to be bleeding but maybe not dying. The animal is breathing hard, smelling the air, listening the same way I am listening. It gives a shake of its great head and I can see steam rising in the heat from its muscles and flesh and hair. It is so *alive*. Even in my fear, watching this deer-beast fills me with such intense joy that I've tears in my eyes. It walks a little further away, elegant and easy despite its size, away from me and into the clearing, head lowering towards the ground.

More movement, coming from the woods behind us. Maybe there are more of them. But the beast, whatever it is, knows what's coming even before I do and is gone.

Skrake.

They shuffle and ooze out of the trees to my left but the beast is disappearing already, tearing off through the grass and within a few strides it disappears into the tree-line at the other side of the clearing. The first skrake follows without a pause but I can hear more now, coming from the trees all around me and I wonder how ever there were so many that I didn't bring them down on top of me. How long have they been following for?

All I can do is cling to my tree and watch as they – four, then eight, then eleven, more – race out after it, stinking and twitching and moving I swear with something that looks like glee. Maybe it's the blood they're smelling, or they can hear it, or maybe they're just following each other, giving each other a direction. I barely breathe and do not move but can see the fabric on my chest vibrate a little every time my heart beats.

The skrake are nearly away, nearly through the trees at the other side of the clearing. Once the last is just out of sight I breathe out and try to unstick my hands from the trunk of the tree and I let myself down as quietly as possible from my branches back on to the ground.

I feel nearly good. If I'd seen something like that just a few days ago I'd have wet myself for sure.

And then I see there's another, a last skrake making after that mad beast behind its friends, and I'm so surprised at the sight of it that I do wet myself a little.

Chapter Eight

I WAS BORN AROUND SUMMER SOLSTICE AND THAT'S WHEN WE celebrate me getting older. Bigger and stronger. In the olden times every day had its own special name, but Mam doesn't know what they were called and if she hasn't them probably nobody does. If there's a nobody out there at all.

We celebrate Maeve's birthday at winter sol, and mine at summer sol, and we'd celebrate Mam's the first day snow fell. I don't see why every stupid day needs a name. They're mostly the same, and that's if you've luck.

The summer sol I was seven was hotter even than usual and I was awake and sweating when Mam knocked on my door and told me to hurry up and shift myself up out of that bed.

'Ready?' Maeve says to me once I'm downstairs, with a not-frown that is her way of smiling.

'To the village?' I ask.

I don't go to the village by myself. It's too far from the house, and there's no point going without them because I'll only have questions. I've only *ever* questions for them and mostly they've silence and warnings to give me back. In the village there are buildings that burnt long ago; there are faded pictures in rotting magazines I'm not to touch, of bright people with snowy skin and shiny hair. There's all kinds of things making promises about different futures, before what happened happened.

'No,' Mam tells me. She's touching the right side of her jaw carefully. The teeth on that side pain her.

'We're going to the woods to celebrate,' Maeve says. She goes whole days barely speaking a word so seven together is a speech.

I pick up the bag that leans against the back door. There's a warm, greasy smell off it. One of the hens was missing the day before but I said nothing. I'm struggling but the weight of it is suddenly lifted away.

'Give it me,' Mam says, swinging it over her shoulder, and Maeve throws her eyes upwards.

We manoeuvre ourselves one by one through the back window and pick our way through the brush behind the house and head north. We stay quiet. The sun is hot on the nape of my neck. Mam and Maeve move ahead of me, quiet and neat, their shoulders nearly touching. Keeping an eye on both sides, keeping an eye on me. I try to copy the way they move, quick and graceful, their feet finding the best place to take their weight.

We are going to the woods, our favourite summer place. The bluebells are long gone but the trees are leafy as they get, and there's a breeze instead of the angry shrill of wind on the beach. It's warm and friendly. The songbirds are singing their little heads off.

We unpack in a clearing at the top of the little hill. There's a chicken, roasted whole over the fire when I was off doing chores, and stuffed with herbs and eggs. There are cold baked potatoes and carrots and rhubarb, too, and a little folded square of paper with salt inside it, and another of sugar. A feast.

My stomach gurgles loud, tight with the hunger, like always.

'Are you famished, little warrior?' Mam asks me, and reaches over to lift back a lock of hair off my damp forehead. Her eyes are smiling because she's watching mine and I can't stop looking towards the bag with the chicken in it. Maeve takes it out and unwraps it carefully; the skin is crisp and brown. It was Speckles. She was old and a bully but my friend, too. I look towards Mam.

'Mam. Mam. Is there anyone else on the island?'

The two of them look at each other for a second. I've asked before but this is a campaign, today: it's my birthday and there's more *give* to them both, a better chance they'll answer me or at least give the usual responses in a new way. And I'm seven, near grown. This is what they've been telling me, that it's time now to stop being a child and that is something to celebrate, too. Maybe it means they'll talk to me properly. The way they talk to each other.

'Did you see someone?' Maeve's voice, hard and sudden nearly like I've frightened her.

Mam is softer always. 'There's no one else here, Orpen, we've told you that.'

'But are there other people on the island of *Ireland*?'

I feel Maeve breathing a bit easier, but Mam is worried.

'We don't know, is the answer,' Mam says in that way she has when she wants to not keep things hidden from me, when she wants to tell me everything. 'We don't know, baby, that's one of the things we wanted to talk to you about.'

'I'm not a baby.'

'No, warrior,' Mam says, with a big, shaky sigh. 'You can grow and read and write and add and subtract. It's time for your real learning.'

'Time for training,' puts in Maeve, and Mam is looking at her seriously and nodding.

Maeve unwraps a potato and sprinkles salt on it. She loves her food as much as I do and she's eating this spud now to let me know I need to get going before my birthday feast is gone. Maeve knows what I'm doing exactly, she always does. She's not a one for eye contact but she's eyeing me now and she doesn't look away and leave me off till I've a mouthful of Speckles instead of questions.

When I open my birthday present it is knives.

Chapter Nine

I'M GONE, PELTING BACK DOWN THE HILL AND THROUGH the woods to where I left Maeve, moving like my life depends on it, which it does.

It's not far but I think about how fast the skrake moved with the beast through the trees, almost on its tail.

This skrake will catch me.

It is bigger than the one I killed a few days ago, a million years ago, and I was stronger then. I can hear it, just behind me, moving with its juddery distinctiveness, on my heels, its dead breath on my neck.

I move faster than I knew I could, but I have come further than I thought and I was away longer than I meant to be. My breath is short and fast, and the muscles in my legs start to ache so I've no more room for thoughts and that is maybe no harm.

It still hasn't got me by the time I run off the path into the lines of shops.

It doesn't land on top of me when my shoe tangles with a branch and I land hard on my front, the little breath I have getting knocked out of me in a rush. My mind clouds with a blank dark of panic for a moment and every inch of my own skin knows that the end has come: for just a sliver of time I feel relief in there, too, but I'm not done yet.

I get up again, Maeve screaming at me, and I move.

Past the buildings, the broken glass, the meaningless rubbish of the roads, and there is where I left the barrow, and for horrifying moments I can't see it but there it is at last and I'm nearly there and thinking that what difference does it make anyway where I am, I'll have to turn and fight this thing – there's no way I can get away from it with the barrow – and maybe I should have stayed in the trees to fight and die. And somewhere beneath my thoughts Maeve is in my ear saying *tactical error* and—

It's on me with not a wham or a slam but something more like an inversion of noise, as if everything in me gets knocked right out. I hit the road hard. It's on top of me and I am flattened. Its rotting elbow is between my shoulders, pressing me hard against the ground, though I can just about twist round enough to get an arm up between us and my face away from its snapping jaw. I'm stuck fast and running out of breath. I try kicking back but can't reach anything. I go methodically as I can, trying not to panic: one leg, then the other, one arm, then the other, but keeping the skrake mouth away from my skin takes nearly all my energy and I'm tired, *so* tired.

In a single moment the weight of it nearly doubles. I can't move at all, can't breathe, and then it is gone and I wonder if this is what happens in the moment before death: a moment of floating, of freedom.

'Get up.' I listen to Maeve in my mind and think maybe this time I'll just ignore her.

'Get up!' She sounds fragile, nearly. She'd never sound that way in my own head.

I clamber to my feet and have to close my eyes against a wave of whiteness; I think I'm going to fall over but it passes. I take two shaky breaths and I open my eyes and it is, it's Maeve.

Actual Maeve. Swaying. Looking like death: looking like someone else entirely. But standing.

'Maeve?' The word isn't even fully out of my mouth before the skrake makes for her again in a blur of movement. She feints left and comes right again to fall into a sort of awkward, too tight fighting stance, waiting and ready and fierce even with her feet almost one on top of the other.

A half-breath later the skrake launches itself again,

talons and teeth for her throat, and she gets her hands up in front of it but goes down hard. It's now I see what is wrong with the skrake, why it never caught me: its body – the body of its host – had been burnt and the meat of the stomach and upper legs has melted and fused.

Maeve is shouting for something. I find it hard to focus, to bring myself back from staring at the fused blackness where flesh had once been. I am removed from everything. I can hear Danger growling.

'Knife! *Knife!*' It's her voice; it has changed, weakened; the deep sonorous tones are gone and it's a rasp. Wind blowing along a beach.

'Knife!'

She is struggling with it. The skrake is much bigger than she is, and though she's a knee up against its chest she has nothing to work with, nothing she can hurt or kill it with, and her hands are got free but her feet are tied still. My hand goes to my knife and I only know about it afterwards because I feel the hilt in my hand and then my feet are moving and since I'm moving I may as well try to be in charge of which way things are going. I take two knives and I put one between my teeth and I put one arm around the skrake's neck and go to pull it off her. I hand Maeve the knife that's in my other hand hilt-first and then I jam my own in the skrake's throat.

I don't stop. I learnt already to keep going, stabbing,

twisting and withdrawing only to stab again, and I don't stop – I do not stop – till the thing is done. I cut with determined fury. I know that Maeve, the bit of her that is left, is watching and now more than ever before I want her to say that yes I am good, I'm a good killer.

Maeve has her legs around what was left of its legs, holding them down, and has one arm into a lock, which is what makes things easy for me. I wrestle the skrake, dead weight now, off her and on to the ground and I try that trick of pressing hard into the small of its back and I keep cutting at it from there. I hear Maeve coughing behind me but I don't want to turn round to face her. This skrake is easier to busy myself with now.

'Muireann?' Maeve coughs again, then retches, a thick, ugly sound.

I feel my heart give a pull and I know I have to turn round and be a human now, which is hard.

Muireann was Mam's name.

I let the skrake go now and sit on the ground a little ways away and then at last go to meet her eyes. She is staring at me, her face red from coughing. There is an expression in her eyes, in all her face, that does not belong there. It is hopeful; she seems young. She is coughing blood up on to the side of the road but she looks nearly happy.

'That one took it out of me. Have we water?'

Numbly I get up and go to the barrow and fumble and

find a half-full plastic bottle. She takes it from my shaking hand and between coughs takes a swig. When she hands the bottle back to me it is bloody and I put it aside.

'Maeve?' I manage.

'Have we far still to go? It's mad but I can't remember.' She pauses, looks around and blinks a lot. She is confused but her happiness shines through it. Her eyes keep coming back to me and my skin prickles.

'I'm thirsty still. That water did nothing for m—' She breaks off into more coughing, her body, tiny now, racked and bent double with the effort.

She smiles suddenly and I see that her teeth have changed, too. They're falling away at the outsides, crumbling and going black, but they're bigger as well.

'You look terrible, Muireann, I'm only noticing.' She grins at me, mischievous. The effect, with her broken teeth and ravaged face, is grisly. 'You're gone too skinny . . .'

Her eyelids seem heavy on her and she sits, falling harder than she meant to, on the road.

I have to be quick.

'Maeve! Maeve. Phoenix City – which way?'

She stares at me, confused, appalled. 'I'll never go back there,' she says. 'Do you hear me?'

It is real, and she knows where it is.

I knew it, I *knew* it was true.

'Which way?' I shout at her. 'Maeve!'

'Muireann, we swore it together, never to go back. Not after what happened to us.' Her eyes fill, and mine with them. 'Let that baby in your belly be a reminder, Muireann.'

My heart is a stone. I know well what that is; I know it from my books.

I knew it always.

'We should keep moving,' Maeve says, her grey gaunt face shaking off the fear and turning hopeful again. 'They'll be on us before we know. Has it rained?'

She takes two shuddering breaths and wipes her mouth with the back of her hand and looks away. The last words are nearly inaudible. She seems to notice for the first time the length of cord I had tied her legs together with. It didn't slow her down, of course, not even a little. I will have to tie it tighter. Even as Maeve leans forwards to look more closely at it, the lines on her forehead drawing together, her eyes are closing. Her arms and legs twitch, a little at first and then she slumps and the twitches get much worse.

'Maeve,' I say, in nearly a whisper. I wipe away the tears and snot running out of me.

Afterwards we stay for a long time on the road and I think about the thing I knew already really, and I think about men.

It's a long time till I remember the squeaky wheel. Danger whines and comes to sit by me, keeping well clear of Maeve and the mess of skrake smeared on the road, a fatty, viscous ooze spreading outwards from its torn proboscis. I've an answer for the wheel at least.

Chapter Ten

MY CHILDHOOD ENDED THERE ON MY SEVENTH BIRTHDAY, and I knew we'd done well to get that much out of it.

Training – proper training with Maeve – gets going. Stretching so I'm flexible, running and swimming so I've good breath, exercises for my muscles. Technique is next and then practice, the top of the triangle that Maeve draws in the sand.

On the beach, I train every day. The ocean is a noisy, angry roar, hurling itself on to the shore like a fist again and again. In the distance are the bones of the whales washed up long before I was born. They're a pure, stark white, monstrous skeletal fingers reaching up into the sky.

The fingers are my goal every day and every day I try get to them a little bit quicker against the wind. I run hard, the morning's coddle making me feel heavy. I pretend something is chasing me, breathing fleshy breath on the back of my neck. It's not hard to put the frighteners on yourself, so it's not. Every day I manage it, I get there faster; my legs lengthen, they want the work of it.

Just beyond the fingers is the rocky sea bridge, and I climb out on to it, past the crashing, crushing waves, to check our pots for anything edible. I find a lumpen, squishy purple thing. *Neither fish nor fowl*, Maeve would say. I hang on to it anyway and sure enough the seagulls start shrieking and following me. They're big birds and smart, but no good to us. I once made a fire and cooked one and took a bite of the greasy, sour-smelling meat. That was me told thrice. 'You've always to find things out for yourself,' was all Mam had to say about it.

I drop the purplish sea creature in the sand to let the birds dive at it and keep walking, back up the little dunes to the grassy knoll. My hand goes easy to my favourite knife at my hip. I toss it in the air, catch it by the blade, bring my hand back past my shoulder on a level with my eye. I point casually with my left hand, nearly like I don't care where it goes but am just giving the bird its due, but my next movement is all the opposite to that. I throw hard, the balls of my feet and my hips and everything arcing towards the target and I know from the hot flash of connection, before the knife has even left my hand, that the shot is good. There's no getting away from my aim, my power when I throw that knife. That heat is one of the only things I really own.

I train. I train harder than they know, even. On the floor of my room, I get through press-ups and with each smooth lowering of my arms I can see underneath my bed, to my collection of stolen things. Objects I can't find out uses for: rectangles of glass and plastic that feel weighty in my hand. There are tin cans, still full, yet to be investigated but it's words I hoard, mostly, wherever I can find them: books that I know Maeve wouldn't approve of from the covers on them; half-rotten and faded magazines pilfered from the village and the other houses. Everything I can find on the Emergency, the last newspapers, anything at all with the word 'banshee' written and in the village is where I find it, again and again.

There are posters.

They're covered in grime, they're hard to see in the dark and dust of the dead little town but I find them; a picture of two people in silhouette, standing with legs apart, and on top it says 'BANSHEES' and then lower down 'FIGHTING FOR YOU'. There are pictures of handsome women with smooth, lean muscles, with their hair short and shaved, wearing black. Their arms are folded and they look out at me with appraising eyes.

I think about these women, out there, fighting for me. I cannot stop thinking about them, even though they'd all be dead.

A picture in a magazine of the faces of the women grouped together and looking out over a wall, shielding their eyes from the sun, says 'VIGILANT FOR YOU'. These words are in my dictionary too, 'banshee' and 'vigilant', but they're from a different world, the world that died. I try to make sense of it and can't and I ask Maeve who tells me to grow up now and stop asking questions and then I ask Mam who says she doesn't know anything about them at all, she wishes she did. I'm not meant to be going to the village by myself is all Maeve says.

BANSHEES rings in my head, and PHOENIX CITY, and HERE FOR YOU. It is all I can think about; the women who were out there once, the women who weren't afraid of the skrake.

Mam and Maeve let me know how good they want me to get by showing me how good they are. They've their own knives on them always, for throwing and one for sawing, and Maeve and me have our own special ones, too, with the gold handle. Mam gave me hers, I suppose. They've staffs as well, and I've mine though in my hands it's only a stick. There are targets all over the island, I see now, ready and waiting for me. I start at three steps out, standing still, and we go from there. When I think I'm getting good they show me what they can do, throwing and catching each other's blades, arcing them to shave hair off each other at ten paces. When they spar it's the same. They work as a team even against each other, with knives or staffs or their own bare hands and feet, showing me how to throw a roundhouse and how to step out of it, how to spin and block and hold and release and surprise and jab and weave, and then slowing it down, breaking it down for me to see.

The runs, the swims in the knife-cold sea, the climbs, the drills – they pile one on the other and more on top of that. At last Maeve draws them together into an obstacle course that builds till it's the size of the island; it shifts and challenges and frightens. I'm tired and sore and hungry all the time. There's no space to think, even, till night-time and I'm alone. Then I can imagine the people, fighting the skrake, out there for us. I stop being scared then in the night, another bit of growing-up done. I start to want to be alone so's I can think.

Mam and Maeve try to keep me guessing, to stop me from getting bored. There are so many things they are trying to keep me from. And all the time they are together, they are a team, and I am the one alone.

I get strong, then stronger again. I mind the chickens and check the traps, so reliably empty that the fullest they ever are is right before I put my eyes to them. I sneak away,

I rebel, I go looking for clues around the village to read and wonder over. I practise with my staff but I love my knives. I make a den in a ruined house on the edge of the estate and there I put those things Maeve calls nonsense and won't let me have; that's where I hide all my banshee pictures so I can look them over again and again. I clean and cook and I run the obstacle course again just to show them, and then off I sneak again when I should be sleeping or drawing water or pulling weeds. I make a secret life with secret hopes.

In the evenings we spar, and I always lose and must not cry or even get cross, not now that I'm properly in training. Mam fights with humour and grace and kindness. She makes me love the fight.

Maeve is cold and hard and unfair. 'Like life,' she tells me.

Maeve makes me good at it.

Chapter Eleven

T HE LAST CHICKEN DIES IN THE NIGHT.

I leave its straggly little body, like the others, at the side of the road. Maeve's voice, in an unlikely singsong: *If you kill it you can eat it; if it dies, say goodbye.* I couldn't have ate it anyway. My stomach feels like a knot of scar tissue drawn tight into itself. I can hardly look at the little feathered body. Our wasted wealth. Danger paws it, takes it gingerly in his mouth.

Don't think about what you don't have, work with what you do.

I must have heard Maeve say that a million times and remembering it now is painful. I miss her, so I do, and I'm scared shitless of her now. Though Maeve's hands and feet are tied fast, still and all, I'd pose no problems for her. If she takes a notion to kill me she'll do it all right.

We move. It is difficult now, being so tired and frayed, to take pleasure in the landscape changing around me, but I try to notice the trees, the vines. I hear a whistling and chattering from far away: songbirds chirping. This might be the last bit of life I get.

We've only one plastic container half full of water left but we can store up more when it rains so I feel OK about pouring some into a cupped hand for Danger. He sniffs and laps. When he's finished I take a little more and throw it on my face, hoping it'll wake me up a little, or help scrub the dirty film that has come between me and the world.

It's not too late, I tell myself. Maeve'll tell me in the end. She'll see how far I've come and she'll have to. Then I try good and hard to stop my mind chattering.

I half walk, half jog on the road, not thinking about things. I don't think about how the dog is only skin and bones. I don't think about the chickens, maybe the only and last chickens in the world, dead now, and I've nothing to offer anyone. If I was ever to meet anyone.

I don't think about how Maeve smells like innards left to rot.

The buildings around us are big, and I'm bewaring them, but I can't avoid them. We're in one of the towns near the city, and though I'm moving faster and the barrow is lighter, the going is slow for all the cars and rubbish on the road we've to work round.

The wind picks up and the rain comes early and hard and we're back into fields and woods. We won't get as far as the outskirts of Dublin today, which I'd say is the direction I'm going if I was pushed to give an answer. It was the biggest city before all this happened; maybe I can camp out not too far in and see what's left of it. There'd be things to read at least.

I push the barrow down an alley and in underneath a huge, cavernous space. I'm too tired to even make sure the building is clear, but we find a small room with a door that closes and we lie down and go to sleep while the storm rages. I sleep for a long time, warm beside Danger.

The silence that comes when the wind and rain are finished is maybe what wakes me up. The night is coming on bright with a nearly full moon, so I take up the barrow again and head back out to the road. I can't sleep more and I won't be any less faint with hunger when the sun comes up. At least if I'm moving I'll get warm.

In the half-light I see more signs: a large red circle with an 'X' in it, drawn messily on a whitish metal background. Another reads 'Dublin: 50 km'. The east is further than I thought, but so close now, already there are more buildings around us, and bigger. I think of the signs I left near the beach to Slanbeg; an age away, a country between us, and from one end of this country to the other I've seen nobody living.

Who were these signs for, the 'X's and the warnings? Can they be so old? I run my finger carefully over the jagged metal, trying to imagine the hands that were here before mine.

We're surrounded now by the remains of buildings, slouching and fallen on top of each other, utterly ending whatever was underneath them. I work our way forwards slowly, eyeing toppling spires and leaning walls. The buildings are so tall I've to let my head roll all the way back to look up and when I do, something pops gently in my neck. There's nothing like this on the island. Whoever lived here built higher and maybe fell farther.

We might be watched from a thousand different places, something might jump out at us from a hundred. Up now in front of us in the middle of the road come barriers made of old rock, metal beams, window frames and glass. I put Maeve down and straighten up, guarding my eyes against the sun, trying to work it out. Beside me, Danger whines, thumps his tail in the dust.

I think I can see a way.

Moving slow I lift up the barrow again and veer back and to the right, through a smashed-away door. Inside the building the air is colder and the quiet so loud my ears buzz with it. There's a doorway through to the next building up and over. The wheel of the barrow crunches on broken squared bits of glass and on crumbled bricks and old yellow paper. I want to stop, to investigate, but mostly I want to run, to spend all my small energy on leaving this silence, these stale enclosed spaces, behind us.

A hole in the floor ahead of us divides one side of the room from the other. I find a long strip of wood, thick and only just long enough and I put it down and, heart leaping from me, I squeeze us on and put one foot in front of the other. I will not look down. We come down the other side, the wood lifting behind us as we go. Through a window to my left I can see we're nearly past the barricade.

It's coming off the other side that my foot slips. Behind us the plank falls, dropping one storey or two or three or the whole way to the centre of the earth: it takes a long time to land and when it does it makes the loudest sound I've ever heard. I feel my feet vibrate with it. There's a rumbling and I am frozen with fear, standing stock still, terrified.

Move

My heart in my mouth—

MOVE

Gasping, pushing furiously, feet skidding in the dust, we move while behind us the ground gives way. Ahead of us, a corner of the building has opened up to the street and I run hard, crouched down, Danger a blur behind me.

I don't stop till we're away, and when we are I lie down,

panting, in the dirt. I watch the building as if it's an animal waiting to make its next move. It seems to slouch but it doesn't fall all the way down. After a little while I get up again, coughing out dirt and dust, knowing I need to move. The noise of that little collapse could bring anything down on me.

It's a long time till we slow down and longer still before we come to a stop, on a slope, when I've no more left to give to the day.

I'm getting fairly close to an edge. I know I am not thinking properly. I'm tired enough to sleep and unless I go back there'll keep on being buildings everywhere. At last I climb in under the nearest roof, shaking with tiredness. Danger's warmth and doggie smell lulls me into dreams of home, of Mam and a soft sun and the scent of lavender.

I am awake, sitting up, my heart jammering. I dreamt something confused about being chased on the beach by bone fingers, but before I can think one proper, whole thought, I'm on my feet.

What remains of the night is quiet. The road behind me seems almost to shine in the moonlight, and I watch it for a moment, standing up straight, rubbing the small of my back, blinking blearily in the cold. It's beautiful, I think, in my fug of exhaustion. The countryside, Ireland, is laid out before me: forest pushing in against the hills, tracks of small roads, now paths, weaving between it like rivulets of water on the beach at home. Little towns are nearly consumed back into earth with trees and vines delicately dismantling the stone works of the buildings. To the east the sky is beginning to lighten and I can make out the city proper beginning.

The moon is so bright that the clouds cast shadows on the ground, and I watch them slide forwards lazily. On the road ahead of us are more signs. I wonder who put them there, and what they used to make them. I imagine the hands of men and women and children, helping each other. My heartbeat has slowed. I could sleep again. I let my eyes take one more long look over the country at my feet and that's when my eyes catch on it, on the road behind us.

A figure.

And then another.

Of all the times I have been afraid since I left the island, this is the biggest and the worst. I cannot distinguish my panic from my deep longing.

'Maeve,' I say quietly, in case she's with me.

Beware people.

I can't stay on my own though, so I can't.

If they're men I will run.

I crouch and watch, my shaking hands hugging my knees. I cannot say from looking at them; they're too far. I wish there was just one.

They are moving slowly away from me.

If they are men I will run; they'll never catch me.

Nearly crying with the fright, I stand.

'Hello!' I shout, my voice like a knife in the night.

They slow, stop. Silence.

'Hello!' I go again.

Nothing for a long time, and then a shout back, and it's a sound I have not heard before, but I know immediately what it is.

'Hello!'

It's a man's voice.

I turn and run.

The barrow is where I left it, full of Maeve and not much else. My hands go to grip the handles like they know what they're doing and my feet won't be outdone. I stop short at the entrance to our shelter and listen for a moment and listen hard and then I move.

I run noisy and slow, my breath coming in grunts and snatches, the barrow jumping and swaying dangerously under my hands. I get moving and I keep moving, and I resist the temptation to look over my shoulder for a long time and I don't think at all.

In my mind's eye, unwillingly, I see the figures again. One small shadow, one large. Were there more, in the shadows, walking ahead or behind? I resist glancing over my shoulder and concentrate on moving, on running, until we are on a rise and it's easier for me to pause and to look back over the road beneath me.

I don't know where Danger is.

The hill has been long and I am badly out of breath. The pain I have in my back, all along the curve of my spine, cuts through the panic of the moment and I try to use that. I still my breath and listen for the dog's paws on the cracked hardness of the road over the sound of my own feet and the *whumph* of where the wheelbarrow wheel meets the road. I hiss his name, hoping for his stupid lollop, a rustle in the bushes, but there is nothing.

Am I leaving him behind? Am I leaving him to the men?

I snatch a look over my shoulder and see them, running hard on the long road behind me. They're moving quickly, faster than I can with the barrow. At last I see Danger, slogging to catch up with me, tail held low.

I need a way to hide if I cannot outrun, a place to ambush, maybe, away from the glare of moonlight on the road. There's a sign saying 'ALL ROADS DUBLIN' and a left, and I take the left. They'll have seen I came this way. I need to find more cover, but the ground all around me now is high and flat and clear of buildings. It's going to be hard to hide.

They're going to catch me.

I can hide Maeve, maybe, put her out of the way. The

road forks and I take another left and maybe it'll be OK, if I can get out of sight. I push harder.

Some foliage has broken through the concrete up ahead on the left before a corner: if they take the wrong turn we might be all right for a while, and either way I'll get Maeve into those shrubs and then get them away from there.

I hear them calling.

Their voices are so close I can almost hear words – the first words I'll have ever heard, other than Maeve's and my mother's and my own stupid ones in my own stupid head.

The bushes scratch my arms, but I'm listening so hard for the voices, for footsteps behind me, I don't feel it. I shove the barrow into the cover as far as I can get it and it turns on its side. Maeve falls out – I think of the limp chicken I threw to the side of the road this morning – and I pause to thrust myself further into the bushes after her. Scrabbling, panting, I grab the handles of the barrow and force it round and over so it covers Maeve's head and torso to hide her, to protect her a little. It's the best I can do; it's all I can do. I shuffle back out on my hands and knees and when I go to straighten the spasm in my back is like a whip.

Still and all, I keep going. I move just like I've been trained.

Chapter Twelve

MAM AND MAEVE DON'T TELL ME THEY'RE LEAVING TILL they're nearly out the door, as if they might be saving me from something by doing it that way. It feels like they're not planning on coming back, like maybe I haven't been good enough or worked hard enough. It feels like I'm being left alone, suddenly and for ever.

It is the hardest part of what they do for me.

I wonder is it difficult for them as well, but Maeve looks happy going. She has that non-frown on her face; her steps away from the house are light and easy. I watch them, shocked into silence. I do not cry until they are well out of sight.

I go to the beach because going back to the house

without them in it, without them just gone outside and off doing something, makes it feel like all the other houses. When I've finished shaking and sobbing on the sand I pick myself up and I go off to do the things they said I'd to get done.

The island takes on a new rhythm; my chores take an age, each one, but the day goes too fast. Before dawn's bloody fingers slip through the cracks of my boarded-up window, I am awake. *When the sun's up, we're up*. Maeve.

The house is quiet only for the constant wind, the *shinaun*, tearing through the grass and the ghost-estate, and the noise of the sea behind it. I slip out of my liner, kick away the heavy covers and swing my legs over the side of the bed. I've a fine big yellow and green bruise on my thigh from sparring a few days ago.

I rub my hand over my hair; it's getting longer, Maeve will want to scissor some off when she and Mam come back.

If they come back.

I stretch out, I get down. The floor is cold beneath my palms and the skin on my arms blossoms into goosebumps. I shift on to my knuckles, breathe deep and get through some press-ups, sit-ups, a handstand for the fun of it. I inhale through my nose and close my eyes, listening hard for the sounds of Mam and Maeve coming home all the while. Hearing nothing. It is good to have somewhere to put the energy, the fierceness in me.

More press-ups, the last ten on my knuckles, just the way Maeve does it. The day throbs its first warmth into the room and my body makes a grubby outline on the wall. I drop to my feet, stretch my arms, and shadow-box. I think about the way the balls of my feet work, how well I can tip and balance on them. Three spinning roundhouses, executed quick, one after the other, energy bubbling along my arms and down through my toes like fire. The last I jump for.

Panting now, I drop for more push-ups, because they're my least favourite and I need somewhere to focus it all. My breath sounds too loud, obtrusive in the quiet. I dress, weapons first, my serrated blade and my throwing knives sheathed and in a belt around my waist, and my spare, the little dagger with the slim gold handle Mam gave me. The armpits on my long-sleeved top are crusty but the smell doesn't knock me out and on it goes.

The shape of the furniture in the not-quite-dark of the downstairs is reassuring. There's the dusty couch, there's the globe and the maps and there's my dictionary, obsessed over, words read and repeated till Maeve told me to *whisht*. There the approved books, read to death and falling apart: *Binti* and *Orange Horses* alongside our *Culpepper's Herbal* and *Complete Gardener*. So many versions of the world, and most of them bad. The men making the decisions and women suffering for them. I've a desperate hunger for something new, for information I'm not meant to have, for something I don't know already.

The hearth is still full of the ash from last night's fire, the coddle in its metal pot hanging over it, but things are mostly clean. Maeve teaches me about germs and how we should be careful of them if we have broken skin. Mam says the root and mint and ginger she carries in her herb pouch don't cure everything. Then Maeve'd mutter to herself they don't cure *anything*. If I had even a small cut Mam'd clean it out, though, and put a mixture on it that would sting like mad, and she'd go saying the sting is the good of it, that's how you know it's working. But Maeve doesn't murmur to herself for no reason, so she doesn't. I was meant to learn something about goodness or rightness or health coming from pain, I don't know what exactly, which is what you get when nobody says anything straight out.

The kitchen is our store cabinet. We plan at the table sitting straight-backed in proper chairs. Mam told me, though, how the oven would work in the olden days, with a gas that was piped in all the way to the island, under the roiling sea. Seems like a lot of trouble when you can just go on and make a fire. Maeve says, *No matter, sure aren't we all paying for it now.* She says it in the voice that means I needn't bother to ask more questions.

I open the presses, our whole store. There's the bottled potatoes, the carrots. There's soap and bleach and toothbrushes still in their plastic. Each brush is a sentence, a symbol of another six months spent here, with nothing changing, only me getting stronger and more restless, the hunger in me growing.

Mam taught me to read and write, and gave me books about doing harm and keeping from harm. Hunting, trapping, fishing, finding water, keeping seeds and growing things, and livestock, and there are pictures of cows and sheep and horses and deer. I'd give blood to see one; I'd go a long way for very little, I'm learning. There're only rabbits and rats to hunt unless you can get a songbird, which I can't, and our only livestock is chickens. Still, I get the idea.

Failing to prepare is preparing to fail, is what Maeve says about that. I'd say she means I'll go with them one day to hunt off-island and I'd better have some idea about it. *Better safe than sorry* is another one of Maeve's rules. Another is, *Remember your Just-In-Cases.*

We've a clock at home and it doesn't work but Maeve used it to show me: facing forwards you'd be looking at twelve and your six then would be behind you. *Three*, she might whisper, and I'd look right. *Watch your six*, she'd say, and I'd turn around. *Beware tall buildings* and *Don't trust people*. Does that include herself I want to say and

79

never do. There's no one else around but Mam. *You're never safe, ever.* There's a load more as well but it's this last one sounds most right to me.

It's hard for me to remember sometimes that Maeve is not my mother as well. I know Mam gave birth to me, I know that she strained through pain and blood and love to bring me into this world and then keep me here with her. But Maeve made me. I'm in there, too, in the neat grooves that have been worked into her face by wind and time and sheer bloody hard work. There's something more than reassurance in her thick, strong body in the house. Her missing ear and her scars are her own or maybe hers and Mam's, but I love them, too. All she ever did was work her fingers to their raw bones to make me strong. Mam taught me about how to live, so she did, but Maeve taught me about how to survive.

When Mam and Maeve come back from the mainland, they are tired. They look older and newer as well, though they were gone for only one long lonely night. They have things we need, like wire for the coops, and oil, and things I have not seen for years: battered tins of food, candles. There's a backpack for me and a book I have not read before. I cry when they come back. I can't stop, I'm so full of relief and happiness and *love*, and they can only tell me they'll be going off again. Mam hugs me tight and she tells me how well I did, that I looked after the chickens and the garden and did not let everything go to rack and ruin.

'What did you see?' I ask them and they look at each other and there's a blankness to their faces. Mam smiles and ruffles my hair and says am I ready for more sparring.

Chapter Thirteen

D ANGER IS AHEAD OF ME AND MY LEGS ARE REALLY
pumping and it feels good, for a minute, to be
stretched out upright again, and to be running. A hundred
paces later, though, I know I'm at the last of my strength.

I slow to a jog, then pause and listen hard to the dark. I
can make out their noises behind me. They don't take the
wrong fork in the road; they must have heard or seen which
way I went. I go from standing to sprinting again, the quick
light *thwaps* of their feet behind me on the tarmac.

The sound his voice made, deep, reaching, is echoing
weirdly down in my bones. It reverberates, it is *visceral*.

Mam and Maeve, they've prepared me for nothing.

I'm near panic but I get as far as the corner and past it

and I dive into the side of the road. I made too much noise but I haven't much in the way of options at this stage. There's loud breathing and feet slapping and then a small figure, mostly shadow in the early morning, comes careering around the corner, slowing when it doesn't see me. I get ready. My breathing is slowing and I'm fully alert. I dig my toes into the ground and I feel for my knives. I draw my favourite, the one right at my hip I've the most use of, and take aim, and I settle better into my crouch. I might have to run again when the bigger shadow comes around the corner, which it probably will, and very shortly. With another crack of pain I get my back a little straighter, pull my knife back to my ear and get ready to let fly.

The small shadow has stopped almost straight in front of me and it – no, I see with a burst of relief it's a *she* – she's peering around in the inky blackness, trying to see me. She must have guessed that I stopped, or else she's waiting for the bigger shadow, the man, to catch up with her. Either way, here's my chance, so I steel myself to aim properly for her face the next time she looks towards me. The placement of my feet, the movement of my body are smooth and mechanical, just like I've been trained.

The knife has all but left my fingers when the shadow speaks.

'Hello?'

Her voice is soft and light, and I realise then how young she is – younger than me. Tall, but a child.

I try at the very last to hold on to the blade but it goes from my fingers. It doesn't hit her hard at least and only hilt first, then clatters on to the road beside her.

My position is gone so I leap forwards, my back crying out in agony. I run at the girl and get to her fast and she is surprised when I shove her. I do it hard and nearly regret it because she's so light she goes flying. I can almost feel her little body being cracked against the road and I hear all the wind leave her lungs and the surprised, pained, childish-sounding cry all in the half-second or so it takes for me to be going. I don't look back but my hands are burning with the puniness of her fragile body.

Now that I am not going to kill her – or not on purpose anyway – I don't have a plan. I'm just running away, because there's a man and because they're chasing me, hoping to draw them from Maeve. Every step I take is another I'll have to take back again. Unless they have knives, I suppose, and my back crawls in readiness to feel one enter it, slice through it, bring me down. In the meantime I may as well keep running.

I hear the child's voice again over the noise of my own breathing and running and I feel relieved. She sounds all right. I strain my ears but can't understand what she's saying over the noise of my own breath. I hear her shout out again, to stop. I can only try to run harder, but I'm so tired, I have been going on nothing for so long now. *Failing to prepare is preparing to fail* rings in Maeve's voice in my head but before the thought has even come out fully I have tripped over my own feet and landed, hard, at the side of the road.

I lie there with my arm under me awkwardly and my feet in a knot and take maybe three breaths before clambering back up to get going again. I think about Mam, how she'd want me to keep going. My heart seems to contract and then go outwards and then, stupidly, tears come. I'm angry about that, but since there doesn't seem to be much I can do to stop them I let them be and concentrate instead on putting the one foot in front of the other.

I know that they'll catch up with me and there doesn't seem to be much I can do about that either.

Keep on to fuck.

Danger appears from nowhere to run beside me, and I won't stop to think about why but I am sobbing now, crying so hard that my whole body is racked, and it makes me even slower. What a failure this is: how weak I am. I'm going slow now, slow enough to let one hand graze against Danger's soft head, and against his wet nose when he lifts his eyes to look at me.

'Good dog,' I try to get out through spittle and snot.

The girl cries out again and I hear the word, full and clear.

'Stop!'

There is such a note of pleading in it that I nearly do. When she calls again, shouting 'Please stop,' in a high clear pitch, I glance over my shoulder.

Then I hear the man's voice again. When he tells me to stop it is like an order and I feel a glorious spike of anger. I wonder if I could kill him and I think if he wasn't with the little girl, the child, I could. I would.

They'll catch me, though, and they'll do whatever it is they're going to do and that will probably be painful, and they'll kill and eat the dog. I'll never get back to Maeve, we'll never get to Phoenix City and she will turn, and no matter how much running I do there is no getting away from that solid miserable fact.

My story will end here and better here than at home. At least I have put my eyes on things, at least I got off the island. I did that much for myself.

There must be one good action left, one choice still that I can make that will have been for the best. I click my tongue against my teeth, struggling between breaths, till Danger is looking up at me again and then I use the hand motion that is meant to show that he's to go on ahead, flicking a wrist off in front of me. He runs a few paces in front of me but then waits till I've caught up again.

Behind me the steps of the man and girl are closer and the girl's shouts, telling me to stop, are louder and more urgent. I try to block them out and flick my wrist ahead of me again. Danger won't leave me.

'Stupid dog,' I hiss out between gritted teeth and I smack him on his oily-haired rump. He runs a little ahead of me and I slow, hoping he'll go further but he only looks back and slows again.

I reach for a knife, expecting to feel the man's fingers on my shoulders every moment. He hasn't shouted again but he has gained on me, outstripping the girl, and his heavy footsteps are just behind me. There isn't a second to lose. There isn't a second to think, which is maybe a good thing. I grip the knife hard and trying not to slow too much lean over towards the dog – my back crying out in pain – and I plunge the tip of the blade hard but not deep into the fleshy part of Danger's shoulder. He howls and leaps away from me just as I hoped he would and keeps going and I watch him and think, *Thank you, thank you.*

I slow and once I've lost my momentum my feet stop knowing how to go forwards and I go down hard. I feel my head bounce off the road: there is a crack like the world is coming apart and a clear lucid moment of nausea while the world explo—

Chapter Fourteen

MAM AND MAEVE COME AND GO WHEN IT SUITS THEM, and when I've time to think, when they're away and I'm frightened and lonelier than usual, even, I dream about getting off the island.

I think about it a lot, when I'm on the course, getting through the running or the swim. I wonder could I crawl all the way to the mainland.

I hear, the very odd time, Mam and Maeve talk about the same thing. There are snatches of conversation; there are times there are cracks in their perfect club of two.

I'd rushed through duties and come back to the house, knowing they'd be out on the island gardening but they were home before me, talking quietly. Wanting to be alone but together, in a way that made me feel lonely.

I can move so quietly, I know the house so well, but even still, I only hear little bits.

'. . . won't be able to make sure she's safe.'

'We're *never* safe. The only thing we can do is be prepared, keep up with her training—'

'No, I said.'

'Muireann. Think. If she's never even seen a skrake, she'll never know what to do with—'

'You're telling me to take our twelve-year-old out to fight a skrake!'

'She's not a child. Think what we were at her age.'

I listen so hard in the silence that out of the corner of my eye I can see the fabric over my chest shuddering with every heartbeat. My palms are sweaty, hearing them talk like this. They go so quiet I don't know whether they're whispering or only looking at each other crossly but it's Maeve that goes on again, her voice so low I nearly can't hear.

'We have to take her. She won't learn otherwise. And we'll be there.'

'She will learn, she *is* learning—'

'She knows nothing. Compared to . . . she should be more grateful.'

'But that's what we brought her here for. A safe life, a better life . . . the best life – possible . . .' Mam is louder as usual, tripping and stopping over her words. 'We left so she didn't have to make the same choices we did, so she wouldn't be *caught* the way we were.'

'We left because you were pregnant and you weren't meant to be.' Maeve's voice is cold and flat. It's a warning voice, but Mam goes on.

'For both reasons. For our freedom and hers. And I know, it's not what we imagined and we thought we'd have more and I want to give her more, to show her more, but it's too much, Maeve, I won't. Let her have another few years still. Let us.'

'That's not a safe choice and this isn't freedom, this is hiding. *We need to find more people.*'

Crouched in the hallway, I dig my fingernails into my arms and think about going in to them. What is said then is so quiet it's hard to hear.

'Other people are only a danger—'

'I know, love.' Said with patience and kindness and like she's heard it before.

Maeve says then a bit more quietly, worriedly, 'We made ourselves so safe here. We need to move, before something happens to us.'

'Out there something *will* happen to us. We might be the last ones left,' Mam answers after a minute, and there's a way that they're silent together that makes me think they agree about that. 'I nearly hope we are. Skrake are only the one danger, love.'

'I know that,' so quiet I barely catch it.

'Even if it's still standing, would you have her make the same choices we made?'

There's another silence and my ears strain through it and I hear the gentle noise of fabric on fabric and lips on lips. I know they've got their arms around each other and it makes me feel happy and lonesome all at once.

'. . . you know exactly what I think we should do if one of us gets it.' That's Maeve. She might have said 'bit', not 'it'. Amounts to the same bloody thing, anyway.

Silence again, and I stay listening till it draws out longer than all the other silences and then is filled with the sounds of them going about ordinary things. I hear the clang of the bucket and the sound of the peeler going and that's the end of that. I imagine asking them but I don't, of course I don't, there's no point asking them anything at all.

If they'd ask me, which they won't, but if they did I'd say Maeve is right. We live in a world ended by skrake and it's irresponsible of them not to have introduced me to one yet. If we were on the mainland it'd be different, we wouldn't be hiding. I could protect them while they got older. This being something I'd read or thought I'd read or wanted to read, or maybe just dreamt. Just the kind of nonsense children think when they're safe in their own homes. I think about their words though, about skrake and about people and, always, about banshees.

That night Mam comes to kiss me in bed. Even though I'm training now, though I've been training these five years, she'll still pretend I'm a child when she's worried. She brushes my hair back off my forehead and I close my eyes and fall asleep, happy and loved and feeling as if there was such a thing as safe.

Chapter Fifteen

I AM MOVING.

Later on. My fingers stretch out, reaching for knives. I hear words through the noise in my head, the rushing noise that sounds like the ocean at home. Deep in my own dark I worry over it. I try to hang on to the noise, to home, but it disintegrates when I grasp for it, or maybe I disintegrate. A little while later I hear a voice that sounds like my mother's. There's singing.

The next time the world comes into focus, I keep my eyes closed against it. The voices are the things that have drawn me. There are three after all. I listen for the man's, and the young girl's, but there is another, a woman's voice. The words take a long time to take shape. I realise that I must be in the barrow. It is not comfortable.

Somewhere in the back of my mind I am listening for, waiting for, the sound of Danger's toenails against the cracked concrete of the road and I cannot hear it over the sound of someone breathing hard, close to me. Eyes closed still, I let my hand fall over the edge of the barrow and wait for the dog to push his wet trusting muzzle into the palm of my hand but he does not. I sleep again.

Maeve.

The name is in my mouth and I am sitting up. There is a yelp and I am dropped. The barrow keels over, and then I'm on the ground, coughing, trying to speak and get up and catch my breath. Nausea and dizziness make everything impossible.

I feel hands on my shoulder and I fling them off, find my feet and get up, manage a few paces before I trip over. My hand goes to my belt and grasps at nothing. My knives. Everything hurts, more than hurts, everything screams at me, but the hot fury over my missing knives is helping.

The three of them talk urgently and I try to focus, to hear what they're saying, but it's so hard. The little girl's voice is quiet but clear and high. I squint against the red sunlight: she is a shadow, and the shadow's hand reaches out to me, too slow to be an attack. She's something in her hand. I breathe in deeply and try to focus. The girl is looking at me with huge brown eyes and clear brown skin and she seems so fresh.

'Here,' she tells me. The way she says the word sounds different; I can't trust I understand what she's saying to me. 'Here,' she says again. 'Water.'

'Maeve.' The word is a croak, my voice too quiet. I bring up my hand not for the bottle but to shield my face from the sun and the movement makes me wince. 'Where is Maeve?'

I expect silence. I expect the quiet that has always followed my questions every day that I can remember of my life to this day. Instead I get all their voices at once.

'We had to leave—'

'You were—'

I want to cry.

'Where are my knives?' I say instead, and they've only silence for me then.

I want to stand but don't trust my legs yet to hold me so I stay on my knees, and I wipe my eyes and look around me. There's grass beneath me, trees and greenery all around me. We're not on the road. I don't know where we are.

I snatch the bottle that the girl was holding out to me and then kick myself a little away from them – they're so *close* to me, it's uncomfortable. I sniff the lid of the bottle while the three watch me in silence. I've never seen water so clear and I drink deep. It's cool and delicious. It helps me think. If they'd wanted to kill me straight out I'd be dead, I suppose. I want my knives badly, all the same.

'I have to go back,' I say. My voice sounds weak and strange in my own ears. I try to make it sound tougher. I try to sound more like Maeve. 'Show me which way.'

The two older ones, the man and woman, look at each other. The woman steps forwards. I see her better now. She's older than me but still young, and she's pale skin and long, whitish hair. It's dazzling to look at, her hair. One hand holds a long pole and the other rests on her rounded stomach.

'There was an explosion. A bang?' She speaks slowly but is impatient with it. Her voice is hard, but not like Maeve's. The way she makes words is so different from the way I do, I nearly think she's something wrong in her mouth.

I stand up; my hand goes again to my belt, my fingers reaching automatically, finding nothing. I feel furious; I feel a little more alive. I've a good-sized stone near my foot and I reach slowly down to pick it up, keeping my eyes on the three of them. I wield it lightly in my right hand and feel satisfaction when the woman puts up a hand and takes a step back, guarding her stomach.

The man steps forwards.

'You're all right,' he says, and his voice is kind-sounding but so deep, and I can feel it vibrating again under my skin. 'Do you understand me?'

I don't bother nod and take another look around me instead. Is it morning or afternoon? Is this the way we came? If I went west now and got back on to the road I'd find her again. The sun is low in the sky, the shadows long.

'How long was I – asleep?' I ask. I can't remember the proper word for what I was, my head is still reeling. My voice comes out quiet but they hear me OK.

'All day,' he says. 'What's your name?'

'Where is the woman I was with?' I say it slowly and carefully and watch them now. The man and the woman look at each other again. He wrinkles his forehead and she does something hard-looking with her mouth.

'Tell me where she is.' I make my voice loud and brave and I lift my stone a little. I look at the woman, and she speaks.

'Dead,' she says. 'She was bit. How long were you carrying her around for, half turned like that?'

'She wasn't,' I whisper, and when they look at me and say nothing, I say it again, louder. 'She wasn't dead.'

Not yet.

The three of them only look at me and each other.

'Where is she?'

The man shifts from one leg to another and the girl turns

to look at the woman, with a little pucker of skin just above her nose. Looking at whole new people, the three of them with their voices and faces and lives, the man, who I've mostly tried not to look at now – it's too much. My legs are having trouble holding me up.

I close my eyes and breathe again. I wish I had my knives.

'I have to go back,' I say, trying to make my voice soft and clear. 'Which way?'

'For what?' the woman says.

In one smooth motion and with almost no thought at all, I throw the stone, hitting the woman solidly on the forehead. She's knocked back, more with surprise than the force, and sits down hard on the road. She stays there, blinking, and a trickle of blood runs down her face from where I broke the skin.

I don't feel too good about that but the man is scared and they've given me time so I grab the girl, who is nearest to me. I pin her arms and move her away from the other two. She screams and the woman cries out, reaches a hand out for the child even while she sits on the road.

'I am going back,' I say. 'You're going to bring me back where you found me.' I'll tear them limb from fleshy limb if I need to. 'Where are my knives?' I shout. The little girl flinches and tries to cover her ears, only I have her arms caught fast.

The man just stands there, his hands up in front of him, motionless. He is panicking. He's no training, I can see that much already.

'Get me the knives, or I will hurt her,' I say to the woman, who is still sitting but doesn't look dazed any more. The girl in my arms is tall but so skinny, so light. Her dark hair brushes against my neck and chin, and her little bones feel brittle beneath my rough fingers.

'Move!' I shout at the woman and she jumps and gets going, moving towards the packs and bags.

'Bring them to me,' I say, and the woman steps forwards.

'Don't!' says the man, moving at last. 'Don't, she'll kill Aodh.' Aid, it sounds like he's saying. I have a name now for this little girl I'm trying not to throttle.

Aodh lets out a small yelp. I wish that the man hadn't said that I would harm her. She's scared enough.

'You're hurting her!' says the woman.

I think about saying that if I wanted to choke this girl, Aodh, or kill her, then she would be dead. This man and this girl would be dead, knives or no knives.

Instead I say, quietly, 'Bring them here. Put them by my feet.'

The woman steps towards me. I glimpse her face and see that she is more angry than scared now. That's two of us.

Anyway, she's not smiling any more.

She stumbles over something, her own feet, maybe, and I flinch, picturing her falling over, the knives piercing her swollen body. I let go of the girl without thinking to step out and put my hands out for the falling woman, just as the man cries out 'Nic!'

The girl, Aodh, hits me, a good whack for someone so small – she's had some practice – throwing all her small weight into a side-kick to my stomach and bouncing off it to get out of my reach.

Even as I step back again quickly to grab my knives, the woman, Nic, gets up. She was faking, I realise, to test me, to get the girl away from me.

It doesn't matter. I'm armed now, and angry.

'Where is the woman?' I ask again. The three have grouped together, holding on to each other. 'I won't ask again.' I say it quietly, the decision breathed into being with the words.

'We don't know exactly.' Nic's tone is flat.

'Where did you last see her?'

'Down that road.' Nic points in a direction and I make a note that it's east. It's definitely the afternoon, then, late afternoon.

'And the dog? I'd a dog with me, a black dog.'

There is a long silence.

'Answer me,' I say, and finger the hilt of my knife in an obvious way.

100

'We don't know where we are,' the child says. She sounds all right, I think with relief. She didn't hurt herself.

No, I mean, *I* didn't hurt her.

'Take me back,' I say, 'to where you found me. I'm not asking.' I put my hand again to my knife-belt.

They are frightened of me.

Good.

Chapter Sixteen

'THIS IS STUPID.' I AM NEARLY GROWN, TALLER THAN MAM now, but I sound like a child even in my own ears. I'm hungry and cross. 'I don't know why we can't go back and get food.'

'We're not on Slanbeg: there's nowhere we can go for food. What you have with you is all you have.'

It had been settled eventually; I was to go with them to the mainland. Before we get this far, even, I am to sleep out with Maeve on Slanbeg, to practise, somewhere safe. Every time I think of the way they threw around this word, *safe*, my fists would curl into themselves till my knuckles went white. I'm older now and wiser to the secrets they keep from me.

'To practise what?' I ask.

'Practise being scared.'

We are pretending that we are on the mainland, that we could be attacked at any minute. I am thinking about roasted chicken with crackled skin. And, always, of being away.

'I'm not scared,' I tell her.

'Don't be a fool,' Maeve says to this. She's trying to go easy on me, I know, but she keeps forgetting. She does try, so she does, if I haven't Mam nearby to soften things for me.

'You have to learn how to be in control of your body,' Maeve tells me. 'Food isn't in control of you. Water is not. The weather isn't in control of you. Not even skrake. Only you are.'

I try to ignore the gnarling of my stomach so that I can think about this, but I'm too annoyed. I'd have packed food if she had let me. I finger the knife strapped to my leg, testing its edge, letting it dig into my skin. Maeve is sitting opposite me, on a grassy tussock to keep her bottom out of the damp bogland. Her legs are bent on the ground, crossed at the ankles with her arms on her knees, her stick balancing. She looks content, actually, happier than she is usually in the house, though she'll be hungry as well.

'Close your eyes and concentrate on one thing,' she says.

'I am concentrating on one thing,' I tell her. I'm rarely so cheeky.

'Whisht and concentrate on something else. Your toe.'

I'm so angry I want to act out, to strike, to get up and walk home. That might give them another excuse not to let me off Slanbeg, though. I'd be here for ever, till they die and I'm alone and then me after them. I could cry, I want so badly to see something other than the island.

'Cross your legs like mine, close your eyes,' Maeve says. 'Breathe in through your nose and out through your mouth. Do it slowly, think about it while you're doing it.'

I look away, and back again. I feel prickles of sweat in my armpits; I am trying to work up to something, to ask her something that Mam wouldn't answer, wouldn't even entertain.

'Maeve.' I know it's useless, but I still have to try. Just in case. And this is soft as she'll ever get with me. 'Tell me about Phoenix City.'

Her eyes snap open and flash on to mine: she is suddenly furious. 'Where did you hear that name?'

I can't tell her I've been secretly picking through debris in the town. *Looking for trouble*, she'd call it.

'I've seen it written,' I say. 'In the village.'

'Cop on to yourself, Orpen, and stop reading nonsense,' she says, getting hold of herself again. 'That's not what Muireann taught you for.'

There's no use, I think, none at all; I cannot make her tell me things she does not want to. But I know, I know

104

nearly for sure, that Phoenix City is a place. Is or was.

We glare at each other but eventually, as always, I do as she says and cross my legs the way she has hers. The rough grass scratches my ankles. My heart is hammering. She is angry, still, though she's trying to hide it. If I dared to ask about banshees her head would probably pop off.

'Concentrate, Orpen.'

I try. We are quiet for a long time, and I think about Phoenix City, but I notice, too, the smell of the air: it is pungent with a healthy, robust wetness. I open one eye a crack to see is Maeve watching me. But hers are closed and she looks calm and unalterable.

'Feel your heart rate slow. Let your breathing slow.' Her voice is quiet and softer than usual. I close my eyes again and breathe in the rich air.

We sit there, in the damp bog, thinking about our breathing.

We're meant to pretend we're on the mainland, which means there'd be something for me to hunt. Maybe I'd see a deer. Maybe we could build a fire. We've been practising, too, where it's safe for a flame, where skrake won't see it, which is almost nowhere, according to Maeve. In buildings sometimes, or if you find a cave.

'Concentrate,' Maeve cuts through my thoughts. 'Direct all your mind's energy to your toe. Don't think about how it looks, how long the nail is, whether it's clean or dirty. Just focus on your feeling of it.'

I try.

'Sometimes your mind will wander,' Maeve says quietly. 'That's fine. Recognise that it's wandering, and bring it back to the task in hand. Practise this over time, and it will wander less.'

We are quiet for a long, long time. Every time I start thinking about my stomach, distracted by the gurgling noises it makes, I try to catch hold of it the way you would a rope and think again about the big toe on my right foot. I think about Mam, pottering about in the empty house by herself and I feel lonely for her, frightened for her, even, but then I shake that off, too.

Time passes.

Maeve's voice breaks in softly. 'Now, imagine your toe slowly getting warm.'

I imagine my cold toe getting hot, and I think it works a bit, though I don't let on to Maeve, and we keep practising. After a long time we switch the concentration to my stomach; acknowledging it empty and then imagining it filling up.

Maeve says to me that we'd be practising this technique a lot in future, and in the end I'd be able to go for days without food without the hunger impacting too much on my abilities.

'We should have done this earlier in,' she says, and I don't know if she means imagining things about my toes, or practising for getting off the island.

Then she does an odd thing. She reaches over and puts her hand on my head in a gentle way, a way she hasn't managed since I was very young. I tense up as soon as she reaches for me, getting ready, but she only takes her hand away and then she smiles at me. It's odd being here with her, without Mam. We spend time together when we're training but not like this.

'Being able to control ourselves,' she says, 'is the essential difference between us, and the skrake, and between us and men.'

'When can we go to the mainland?' I ask.

'A little while yet. Your mam and I will go again before we do.'

'Why, why can't I go with you?'

'You know why.'

I don't answer and look away to hide the wetness of my eyes.

'The skrake are dangerous,' she says. 'We want to make it as safe as possible, that's all.'

'And what about people?' My voice is stiff but I want to ask all the questions I might get answers to now, since she's talking.

'They're dangerous, too,' she says, and I think I'm

probably lucky to get that much out of her, but then she goes on, 'Men are dangerous. But we've been looking,' she says. 'Sleep now.'

And I do. I fall asleep, which goes to show how frightened I was, I suppose in the end, which was not at all. Not with Maeve beside me.

Chapter Seventeen

THE NIGHT IS STILL CLINGING ON TO THE WORLD AROUND me and dawn is muddled and unrealistic. I am awake, shivering violently.

In the dark my head felt too heavy for my neck, like a boulder trying to balance on a stick. I fell asleep, woke up sweating, and slept again. It was a mistake, training would have it, falling asleep. They could all have got away in the night, leaving me here with no supplies – I have no idea where my things are now, my bottle and blankets, and no way to find Maeve. Sick like this, I'd probably die.

I could always die.

In the morning, though, nothing has changed; they're still here, fast asleep. That's dangerous, feeling like I can get away with things. I've been trained better than that.

My thoughts feel far away from myself.

I know Maeve is out there, under a bush.

And beyond her somewhere, Phoenix City, still.

The three bundles in camp are motionless. I watch them, cuddled together for warmth, wrapping my arms around myself. After our discussion they settled down, all together. Nic is sleeping in the middle and one of the man's hands is thrown across her belly, and I think about that for a moment. I wonder is that how Mam looked once, and did a man ever throw his arm over her, to claim her in that way. The child has a rock in her hand, but her fingers are limp and all three are gone, fully asleep. They look like a family, a unit.

It's idiotic to sleep like that in the open when there are skrake around, and me, to harm them. I've maybe never slept like that, so soundly, so *out*. Where do they come from that they can sleep like that?

I close my eyes and try not to move. My limbs hurt so much that I'm worried I mightn't be able to walk the road – not for long, anyway. The day warms as the sun comes up and I stop shivering and a little while after that I sleep again.

It takes a few moments to come to where I am. Blinking hard against the sun, I look around me, my neck giving out and then everything else joining in, my back especially. I feel a wreck, a ruin.

'Morning.' The man's voice. The three of them, woman, child and man, are twenty paces away, all staring at me.

I get to my feet, wincing in pain, one hand dropping to my knives.

'Give it a goddam fucking rest, will you?' The woman's voice cuts through the space between. 'What the shitting fuck is your issue? We saved you, you outlying sack of—'

The man puts a hand out and she looks at him and closes her mouth and turns away, but she can't keep her mouth shut for long. 'If we wanted to hurt you, we'd have hurt you.'

I know this myself, but they could change their minds any time they felt like it. Everything changes, and when things go they go pretty fast in my experience.

Don't trust anyone.

Maeve. Of course.

Where is she?

'Where is she?' I say, my voice like stone, dead and hard and not interested in arguing.

'What's your name?' the child asks.

I say nothing.

'I'm Aodh,' she tells me in her bright voice, 'and this is Cillian, and this is Nic.'

I want to tell her to keep her voice down, it's dangerous talking like this on the road.

'Don't you have a name?'

I say nothing yet but lower my guard and begin a stretch on my right, rotating my arm at the shoulder slowly to see what works, but then stop. It's too hard. I'm still cold, but sweating, too.

'I told you,' the woman – Nic – is saying.

'That's not very nice,' says Aodh, but I don't know who she is saying it to. I keep my eyes on the horizon.

'There's no point talking to her. We should have just let her be.'

'She'd have died in the minefields.'

'Yeah, we should have let her. She's no use, she'll die anyway. She's gone in the head.'

'Where have you come from?' I ask quietly. My voice sounds alien to myself I haven't used it in so long, but they don't hear it they're so busy chatting to each other. I've never heard so much talk.

'Hey!' I say, louder, which makes my head pound. They quieten down and I repeat myself.

Nic and Cillian look at each other and then at me.

'Phoenix City.'

It feels nearly like being socked one in the stomach, right in that sweet spot under the sternum. I can't catch my breath suddenly and I feel faint. The blood rushes in my ears.

'Are you all right?' The man.

I breathe, try to think. 'It is real?'

'Yeah, it's too fucking real,' Nic says, not looking at me.

I shake my head. It's hard to think around the pain. I focus on the most important thing, the one thing I know. 'You need to take me to where you found me, to where . . .' It's so hard to say *Maeve*, or *body*. 'To where you found the barrow.'

Nic lets out a sound, a hard noise that I realise is meant to be laughter. Cillian doesn't take his eyes from me. Aodh watches all of us, chewing her lips.

'We can't go that direction,' the man says, and there's something in the way he says it that is meant to sound like a decision has been made already and that's that. It makes my fingers curl in anger.

'I'm going that direction,' I tell him, narrowing my eyes, 'and you're coming with me.'

Aodh walks towards me, slowly, keeping her eyes on me and I wonder is she going to attack me. I shift my weight, holding the foot that hurts most a little off the ground. Injured, tired as I am, I worry I don't have the control it'd take to keep her away from me without hurting her. She stops a few paces away and holds out what she's carrying to me.

I'd never take it except for the way she says, 'It's OK.' Her huge eyes are full of worry. I snatch the bag off her, take an unbalanced step back, nearly fall and manage not to. I keep my eyes on her, and on the others, as best I can.

The bag is full of liquid and I realise then how thirsty I am, how weak for lack of water. I bring it to my lips and drink. What meets my lips is not water; it's something cold, sweet. I spit it and throw the bag on the ground.

'Poison!'

Aodh steps over to pick it up, wipes it off and, calmly, drinks long swallows. She keeps her eyes on me. Then she offers it again, burping loudly. I think about it. Take it. Drink. I can nearly feel the sweetness reaching out into every part of my body that needs it, my arms and legs and toes. My head. I drink till there's nearly none left in the pouch and I only stop because I don't want to finish it on them.

'Are you hungry?' Aodh asks me. I don't answer. It feels like a weakness to say that I am. I don't know what it means, to take their food.

'I have to find her,' I say again. Angry, but not so angry.

Nic and Cillian are stepping closer to me, which makes me uncomfortable. I try to back away again but my feet are making things difficult for me. I badly want to sit down.

'You can't walk,' Cillian says. 'Even if we wanted, how would we take you?'

'The barrow,' I say.

'Well, we're not taking you in the barrow.' He says it in that same voice. 'Look, you're not from Phoenix City, are you?'

Instead of answering I glance around. We're being too loud. I need to get them to go easy, go quiet.

'Take us to where you came from,' Nic says.

'Take me to where you found me.' I'm trying to think how to force them. I can, I think. So just shut up and take me.

'We saved your life, you know,' Nic says. 'That mine would have killed you, blown your legs off.'

I can make no headway with that.

'Tell us your name,' the man asks.

'Keep your voice quiet,' I say, and then I ask the other thing I need to know. 'Danger?'

They look at one another again.

'The dog. A black dog. Followed me everywhere.' I don't know where the tears come from but they itch and prickle and then run down my face when I blink. Nic meets my eye and shakes her head. I look away. I knew already that he was dead. If he wasn't dead he'd be with me. Those were the only two options for that dog.

Aodh comes closer and I let her. I'm not afraid of these people, I decide once and for all; it's them should be afraid of me. I feel flesh on my hand and see that the child has taken her fingers and put them into my palm. I shake her off and blink away the stinging in my eyes.

'Take me to where you found me,' I say. 'And then I'll go with you. I don't care about what we do once we find her.'

115

This is true, I think. Mostly true. I want to see Phoenix City still if it stands, I want to be safe. But Maeve is the thing, the only thing that matters. I don't tell them that if they argue with me I'll make them do what I want. I don't tell them that my feet, my pain, means nothing. I'll hurt them if I have to, even the girl.

'My name is Orpen,' is what I do tell them.

Chapter Eighteen

I WATCH THE WAY MAM AND MAEVE PACK CLOSELY THIS time, Maeve's staff and Mam's knives no further away than their fingertips. They do it the way they do everything else, the two of them moving together, a team, a world unto themselves. I feel already small stirrings of the panic I get when I'm alone here.

'We'll only be gone a night,' Mam says. 'Then it'll be the three of us packing up to go.'

I want so badly to say to them to take me now, but I've said it a million times before and I stop myself. Mam hears it anyway.

'You are coming with us, all right? We've agreed. Next time.' There's a sharp edge to her voice; it's rare enough for her. She doesn't want to let it happen, even still, she wants me to stay here on the island. It was Maeve talked her round.

'We've not stayed overnight anywhere near the coast in a while,' Maeve says now, her voice trying to be softer than Mam's and failing. It's strange, to see her try to explain things when my mother won't. 'We want to call over and make sure it's OK for you to come next time. We'll be back before you know it, this time tomorrow.'

I help; I bake spuds and wrap them up with apples from our store, and boiled water in plastic bottles I've scrubbed with hot water and soap. Truth is, they could be gone days with no food and it'd be no bother to them.

I watch them pack, so calm you'd never know they weren't just heading off out to feed the hens or to the woods for the afternoon. They've such control when it comes to this island, and themselves, and they've no fear of Ireland. Love wells up within me and I bunch up my knuckles to fight down the feeling so it doesn't show. I'm more scared than usual, even, but what harm? What difference? Anyway, if they're not scared of getting off Slanbeg I shouldn't be either, or afraid of staying on my own. Not this time.

'Do you know exactly where you're going?'

'What will you do when you get there?'

'What will I do if you don't come back?'

These are the questions I do not ask because I know Mam would sigh and say nothing and Maeve would nearly growl. There is so much we cannot say in this house. There is so much knowledge I cannot have.

'Come down with us,' Maeve says, nodding to the packs.

I keep my thoughts to myself, watching them move easily towards the water. I try to be like them but I can't be, I've no pal the way they've each other. I've nothing to work with.

The old barrow with its big wheel is handy for hauling their packs down towards the water. I drag out our sturdy little boat, hidden in the trees, to the water. A skiff, they tell me. Maeve ruffles my hair and Mam pulls me close to her for a hug. I allow myself one big breath of her, then wriggle free when I feel the tears start up. I help them push off and I smile at them till I'm sure they're away.

Alone, I walk through the village. The whole island feels different without Mam and Maeve on it; the silence is so aggressive. The noises, from the wind or a bird, are threatening. On my left now is the big shop. I've been inside it before and know there's nothing good left. After the Emergency something went badly wrong inside. You need a torch to see anything, but there's only bones covered in stained and smelling cloth. When I was a child I was fascinated by the death in there, the battle that had been.

Beware people. Maeve. That was all she'd to say on the matter.

And being alone, I add for myself.

Outside, back on the main street, I walk slowly on, kicking weeds and plastic and mouldy paper out of my way. The road beneath my feet is rough. The hard blue surface is split and uneven, giving way. Weeds grow through the cracks, some as high as my waist.

At the top of the little rise I look to the east. From here you can see what remains of the old bridge, a long road over sea between our island and the mainland, built with cement and steel and wire. It used to stretch the whole way to Ireland, and even now it's packed full of cars, like massive dead beetles, relics from a time long past, all quiet and finished but not a single one empty. The cars are mostly facing towards the island. Everyone thought a little place like this was a good idea, across water, away from the cities and towns. The bridge is ruined, chopped in half by something so big, something disastrous.

I watch the curve of the ruined bridge run straight out into the sea and hold up my hand against the glare of the sun. I try to catch sight of the skiff, but it is gone.

Chapter Nineteen

NIC IS TRYING TO GIVE ME SOMETHING.

'Put this on your face. And your feet, probably.'

I don't know what to do with it so I don't take it off her.

'The sooner you heal, the sooner we can get out of here.' Nic glances at Cillian. Aodh sits a little ways away, drawing in the dust and humming, but watching us as well. Nic reaches for me and I flinch, my hand dropping as ever to my knife-belt.

'Stop, would you,' she says quietly, taking my foot, my worst foot, and studying it. 'You need a load of rest is all,' she says. 'Aodh, bring some water, good girl.' The two of them together clean my torn-up feet and put something on them and wrap them tight in cloth from their packs.

The whole time Cillian is pacing, shielding his eyes from the sun and watching the horizon. I'm glad someone is as worried as I am about the skrake. We've been in one place, making too much noise, for too long. We are on borrowed time here.

Cillian keeps his eyes on me but says nothing. I watch him back; it's hard not to stare, everything about him being so foreign.

Maeve is abandoned, dead or dying, and with every moment I sit here more skrake might gather to overrun us.

'We need to move,' I say.

They agree between them that Cillian will stay with me, and that the others will go on, head west, staying on the road and getting as far as they can. We'll catch up with them.

It's all a stupid idea but the man says this is the way it'll be and I wouldn't listen him but Nic and Aodh do. There's not much I can do about it and I don't try too hard; dealing with one will be easier than three. We grew up in different worlds, these people and me. Theirs kept them safe a long time and they trust it the same way I trust my training. I know I'm right but I haven't the words to say it to them, and as long as someone can show me Maeve it doesn't matter.

'I don't know if this is true where you came from,' Nic is saying to me. Her face is quiet and she keeps her eyes fully on mine. She's a cloth and she's rubbing off the stuff she put on the little cuts on my feet none too gently. Cillian and Aodh are taking things out of their packs and putting them in again. All the touching and help and eye contact has me feeling uncomfortable. I look about anywhere but back at Nic.

'In Phoenix City there's a code amongst women. We look out for one another, we take care of one another if we can.' She won't leave her eyes off my face. 'You seem . . . you've been out here a long time. But you've survived. You carry your dead, I don't know why.'

She looks down and the moment her eyes are off mine I feel free to look at her again and I do, taking in her pale skin and red lips and the lightness of her long hair. 'I want to be able to trust you,' she's saying. 'That you're not going to kill him or let him get killed. You'll bring him back to me, won't you? You'll come back.'

I say nothing but I force myself to meet her eyes. A long moment passes and I've nothing to say to her: I can barely understand what she's trying to tell me. It's partly the way she speaks and partly the way I feel and partly the language of it.

'I need him.'

I glance at her belly. 'Is he a father?' I ask, not knowing if that's the right word exactly.

Nic looks away, rubbing her stomach softly. 'I wish it was him,' she says, and as I watch her eyes fill up with tears. She rubs them away with the heel of her hand and I feel a pain, deep and sharp, in the middle of my chest.

'I'll bring him back,' I tell her, and regret it and don't regret it all at once.

'Do you have to go?' Nic tries one more time. 'There's nothing you can do for your – for the woman.'

I don't bother responding to that but say again, 'You should come with us, we should stay together.'

She shakes her head. 'Cillian's right, probably.' Then she's getting up, arduously, and when the man sees her he comes over to help her. I sit in the dirt and keep watching while he puts his arm around her. Their heads are close together, the way Maeve and Mam's used to be.

Watching them say goodbye to each other is hard. 'I'll find you,' I hear him say. Nic blinks and a tear squeezes out over her eyelid. Cillian's thumb moves across her cheek and I look away.

He goes to hug the little girl, hunkering down so he can put his arms around her. 'I love you, kid. Watch Nic for me, OK?' He squeezes her hard, kisses her hair, and stands to walk away from them quickly, shouldering his backpack and not meeting my eye. I look around for the barrow and find it keeled over on its side, the way we left it last night. I rummage and find a half-full bottle of water and a large, smelly knitted jumper that belongs to Maeve. I don't want to rely on anything they have, so I pick up the tipped-over barrow and throw these measly things in it and take off after Cillian. All the time I'm half listening for Danger and every time I don't hear him I remember what's happened and I feel again like crying.

We get moving. When I look back, Nic and Aodh are watching us, holding each other's hands.

He goes so fast I have to concentrate to keep up. My feet are numb, I'm light-headed and sweating and my throat is rough. I slow to take a slug of my own water, dirty and warm, and have gulped half of it before I think to stop.

I move on faster then, wheeling my barrow, nearly on Cillian's heels. We don't talk. I pull the barrow behind me for the relief of walking in his shadow. My back feels broken.

Quiet your whisht, Maeve tells me, *pull yourself together*.

We walk for a long time and I'm lulled, nearly dozing, with the rhythm.

Cillian stops suddenly and I knock my forehead against his back, clip the barrow against the back of my legs, and fall so that I'm sitting in the dirt with my legs splayed awkwardly around me. I see spots.

Cillian hunkers down to dig around in his pack.

'Here,' he says, holding out something that looks like a piece of flattened wood. 'Eat.'

My stomach gives a great empty rattle on cue. I take it

from him and sniff it. It doesn't look like food and it doesn't smell like anything.

'What is it?'

'Food. Eat it.'

My jaw feels stiff when I open my mouth to bite the wooden stuff. My teeth sink into it easily and I chew and swallow. It is not unpleasant. Cillian watches while I eat a few more mouthfuls. My eyes are so heavy then that I can't keep them open and I put my head down on my arms for a few minutes.

I'm not sure how long Cillian lets me sleep but when he shakes me awake I still feel exhausted. It's only when we get going that I realise my headache has let up, that's why I feel so light. My thoughts are easier to get to, and I remember to keep an eye on the landscape, to listen out for whatever's coming next. I walk just behind Cillian. I'm afraid of letting him at my back.

Cillian doesn't look at me and isn't interested in talking now. He is strung tight. He should be, I think. I always feel like I'm going the wrong way; it's nice to know I'm not the only one.

I've trouble understanding what's going on in the heads of any of them, so I do. After knowing nearly every thought that passed through Mam and Maeve's it's like suddenly being blind. Even apart from feeling weak and sad and afraid at being put alone with a man, it's *uncomfortable*.

I miss Mam and Maeve suddenly so hard, so thoroughly, I feel faint again. I try hard not to think about their voices, talking quietly at home in our ghost-house.

I need to know everything about Phoenix City and how far we are and what happened last night, but it's nearly all I can do to keep up and try to make sure the countryside around us is clear and safe. I thumb my knives. I put one leg in front of the other. I breathe deep.

Cillian is waiting for me to talk. He can't know how well I can hold my silence.

We've been walking a while and I'm watching out for my own tracks from the day before in case I can see them – the snaking track of the wheel barrow, my own two feet behind it – and again half listening for Danger and half waiting for Cillian to speak. When he does it's a surprise, the sudden deep voice next to me.

'So. Where are you from?' he says at last. 'How are you out here, on your own?'

I keep walking. It's hard not to say anything but I squint my eyes against the glare of the sunshine and on I go quietly.

'I knew you weren't from the city. I knew you were an outlier, the moment we saw you.' My thoughts trip on this word, 'outlier', but he keeps talking. 'There is a lot we could learn from each other.'

Beware beware beware, I'm thinking, my senses like a

127

string pulled tight. I have to be ready, to fight or run or kill.

'You must have seen a skrake, being out here?' He's talking like he's sure I want to listen to the noise of him. 'The way you grew up, you must have. They tell you in the city that the country's crawling with them, but we've not seen one yet.'

I stay quiet, and hope that he'll talk more, but he keeps his lips closed for a long time. I think again about how the way he says words is so different from the way I say them. The rhythm sounds wrong.

'So look, after we find her, once we've met up with the others, where next for you?' he asks me. His voice sounds different now, deeper, and he says the words more slowly. I glance over at him and he's looking at me closely as we walk. 'Back to your little hideaway?' The way he looks at me makes me feel like he needs something from me that I don't have to give. I look away and he sighs. He tries again, speaking slowly and clearly, making his accent sound even more pronounced.

'Somewhere there are no skrake?'

I look away and I think about home. The house with our things, the magazines full of nonsense hidden under my bed. The white fingers on the beach. Maeve's room, quiet of her now. I think about her bed, carefully made with her sure, firm movements, with the sunlight streaming in on the soft coverlet from the window. I think about Danger's wet nose and the way he'd put his head to the side and prick up his ears when he was waiting for me.

I blink hard.

'You tell me about the city.' My voice comes out like metal. Why, why were they running, what do they think they'd find out here only loneliness and death? They don't know anything about Ireland.

He's quiet for so long that I think maybe I shouldn't have asked him, ordered him so simply, but then he gets going.

'I used to think living in the city was the only way,' he says, his voice bitter and hard. 'You know. Fighting for the cause. Every year, though, it just gets worse. People are going hungry now.' It sounds like he's thinking of a way to put things, even in the silence. 'The women have the two options, and they're not good ones but men have only the one.'

'Options?' The word is out of my mouth before I can stop it.

'Breeders and banshees.' The way he says it makes me think it's a phrase he's heard a million times before, but I can't take it in. My heart is in my ears and eyes suddenly, my hands are shaking.

Banshees.

Chapter Twenty

M Y MOTHER DIED FIRST, THAT YEAR I WAS TWELVE. They're meant to come back on the afternoon of the second day and they do not.

I wonder is it a test, a new way to be tried and wounded? In my worst thoughts I imagine them deciding to stay off away from me.

Walking back to the house in darkness without them from the beach on that second day, my heart pounding, I flinch at every noise. I am not prepared for this, I think, and I get to wondering how long I'd last here alone, and then how long I'd *want* to last here. I fall asleep in my mother's bed, which still smells like some sweet herb, like lavender.

I'm angry as well, I'm *furious* with them.

I tell myself that they'll be there when I wake up in the morning. We'll kill a chicken and eat dinner and tomorrow night Mam will brush the hair back from my forehead so she can kiss me good night. And then we'll all leave Slanbeg together, a family.

I spend a bad night listening for them in the darkness.

In the morning they still haven't come home.

When the sun's up, we're up. I get through press-ups, sit-ups, I practise my favourite strike techniques in the cold, empty house. I feed the dog and the chickens, and try to read, and think about settling into my secret camp to look at the old maps and think about banshees, or going to the village to see is there anything I haven't looked at enough yet. I do not have the concentration – I need to keep moving.

Instead I run the course. Back out to the beach for stretches in the cold morning air, then a run, out fast to the fingers. Off up then into the woods to climb the tree Maeve marked and down again towards home, sneaking through the old abandoned houses I know so well as if I don't know them, as if they're infested with skrake. In the last, Maeve has drawn the outline of a monster on to the back of a wooden bookshelf in mud and oil; I fling my knives, two to the body, one to the head, a killer shot, so Maeve'd say. My breath coming fast in the solid silence of the ghost-house.

I trace my fingers over the drawing of the skrake, trying to find the shapes of the fingertips that drew it.

When the light is gone and there is nothing else for it, I turn my feet towards home. In the bathroom, with a precious candle lit, I wipe away the dust off the mirror and look to see can I find Mam in my own face; anything of her kindness or softness. Instead it's mostly Maeve looking incredulously back at me.

The day after that I start thinking about going after them.

It's the day after that they come back.

As soon as I see them I know that home is not home any more. It's that day I learn that home only exists in the past. It's that day our house becomes haunted like the rest.

Chapter Twenty-One

I WOULDN'T HAVE RECOGNISED THIS PART OF THE ROAD. I SEE it now, in the distance, the fork and then the lift up the hill. I stop to hunker down and breathe carefully. I close my eyes and concentrate on not wasting the food, the pepcho, that Cillian gave me. The word 'banshee' is still echoing in my head but I can't focus on it now. I need to think of Maeve.

Once this is done the world will change into something sadder and lonelier and scarier. We'll never be as close again as we are now, Maeve and me. I'll be on my own, properly and for good.

I finger my knife.

Beside me Cillian is tense and alert: he's watching the

hills around us, and starts every time the wind rustles through the bushes. He's trying to look out but he's no good at it, he's not still enough. Mostly what I can hear is the blood sloshing belligerently around between my ears.

This might have been a crossroads once, I see. Two smaller trails, one leading left and the other right, down a hill, can just about be made out, and there are signposts. I'd noticed that dimly, coming along the road: there are only signposts where roads meet. That's how it would be, once, long ago. You'd go along the road and could assume you were heading the right direction but every now and then you'd come across another road and be reassured by the world around you, by the safety of a country that was organised to help people. You'd have a family and a community and a government all in place to help keep you going the way you were meant to be going, and now all we have is one person meeting another and trying not to be killed or have to kill.

I can see four signs, all pointing in different directions, and one big one, too, half overgrown with ivy. They were green once – you can see it around the edges – but they're a reddish-brown now. They have been drawn over with some brown stuff, and then symbols have been scratched over them. There are shapes I can just make out, the snake with the cup you see everywhere, but also a circle with an 'X' in it again and beside it a circle on its own. There are words, too: a 'TURN' and 'NOT SAFE' and 'HE JUDGES'. And 'PHOENIX CITY RISES'.

I breathe in and out through my leaking nose and close my eyes. I won't throw up and I've the crying under control. I'm OK. Cillian is watching me, nearly twitching with anxiety.

'They were drawn in the olden days,' he says.

'The words?'

He's looking at me closely, thinking hard. I can't tell at all what's going on in his head and that blindness to what he's thinking is disconcerting all over again. I'll never know people again the way I knew Mam and Maeve, I think, and tears start up prickling my eyes again.

'Do you have those letters?'

I blink at him, confused.

'The signs,' he says. 'The words, do you know what they mean?'

I stare at him. 'Don't you?'

'Educated,' he says, quiet, and then louder he points and asks, 'What does that say?'

'It says we're near Dublin,' I tell him, and since we're talking now, since I've stopped crying, more or less, and he's nearly stopped shaking with fear and anger at me for dragging him back here, I ask the question I need to ask. 'Tell me what happened.'

Cillian's expression changes but he's still edgy, still

trying to keep eyes all around us. *Two lookouts are better than one*. Maeve.

'I'll tell you as we go,' he says. He steps towards me and holds out a hand. I'm not sure what he means by that gesture, but after a worried moment I put my hand out towards his. He grasps it and helps pull me to my feet and I marvel quietly. If Maeve had ever put her hand out to me it would have been a test, an attack.

It's nice to feel a hand in mine.

Once I'm up he lets go and starts walking fast. I bend and grasp the handles of the barrow and move quickly to catch up.

'We left Phoenix City three days ago.' He stops for a moment to look back at me, to wait for me to be beside him and then says, 'It feels longer. Come on.'

I think about this for a moment. I'm not sure any more how long I've been on the road. 'Where is it?' My heart in my mouth; the question I've always wanted answered more than any other, the reason I carried Maeve the whole way across the country. One of the reasons.

'In Dublin,' he says. 'It used to be called Phoenix Park. You can follow the signs to that.'

That's why it wasn't on the map, it wasn't a city before. But I'd have got there anyway without her, I was going the right way exactly, into Dublin. I needn't have even brought Maeve. I could have done the thing I was supposed to do and come across Ireland without her. She could be resting with Mam; I could've buried them together.

I've stopped dead in the road, breathing hard. I think again that I'm going to vomit after all, and then I do.

'Why did you leave?'

After I've thrown up the food that's been given to me, rested for a long time with my hands on my knees at the side of the road, and counted to a hundred I am able to get moving again. I'm light-headed and weak and I still want to cry a lot but beside me Cillian is loud and impatient and frightened. I'm asking him questions nearly to keep us moving, to keep both our minds off other things.

'I told you. There's no living there.' His voice sounds as if it's being strangled when he says this. I wonder do I need to prod him more but he goes on by himself. 'We left three days ago, Nic, Aodh and me.'

'Is she your daughter?'

'She's Nic's, but she feels like mine, too. She's smart, that child, she's special. You should see her with a knife, already. After we got out we ran. It's stopping that's dangerous. And going back . . .' He stops to shake his head and for a moment I think he's going to cry. It is alarming. Instead, though, he gives his head a small shake and says, 'We saw you, on the second day, yesterday. At first we thought you were one of them, but there was the body.

Nobody from the city would ever do that. So we knew. You're an outlier, aren't you?'

Maeve was my pass after all, I think. She saved my life again. My stomach clenches.

'What's an outlier?' I think I know, but I want to hear everything he has to say.

'You know, a person from the outlands. Someone not from Phoenix. We've heard stories but . . .' He moves his shoulders up and down and I think he expects me to know what this means. 'We hid while you passed us on the road. We watched you. Nic didn't want to stop, she didn't want to turn round, but you were heading straight for Phoenix City. Straight for them. Carrying a dead woman, and with a dog. So we followed you.'

'Why didn't you leave me go?'

'You were running straight to Phoenix City,' he says again, with a different tone.

My mind stumbles over this but Cillian is still speaking quickly, huffing out breaths as we walk quickly along the road. 'You're from somewhere else. And that means that you've survived out here on your own. You know how to, how to keep ahead of the skrake and to find enough to eat . . . And maybe there were even more of you. Maybe you have a little village somewhere. Maybe there are others? Somewhere safe.' His speech is urgent and always too loud.

'No,' I say quietly. I feel dizzy. 'That's why we were running.'

'How did you survive out here, all on your own?'

'I'm not alone,' I remind him, and my voice comes out broken and too loud. I slow a little. 'What happened?'

'I told the others that maybe you could help us,' Cillian says, panting.

He wipes his lips with the back of his hand and scrunches up his eyes to look at me. I keep moving, eyes straight ahead, but I watch him out of the corner of my eye.

He rubs the back of his neck. 'Nic didn't want to, but Aodh knew you were heading straight for the minefield. She took off after you to save you and I followed her, and Nic came after us.' He moved his shoulders up and down helplessly. 'It was Aodh saved you.'

'Quiet,' I tell him, wiping my nose on the back of my arm and trying, trying to pull myself together. 'Speak quietly. What's the mind field?'

'The minefield. Where they buried mines. Do you know what a bomb is?'

I nod.

'It's an underground bomb. You can't see it, and when you get near it, it explodes. It'll kill you, it takes your legs off and leaves you bleeding to death.'

The things people do to each other.

I imagine the barrow rolling on to a bomb that I couldn't

see and everything going up. Lying cut in half on the road, Maeve gone, Danger gone. And then dying. It doesn't feel that different from where I am now.

This is what happens when I try to save things: they just die worse.

'And the dog?' I have to ask. I have to be sure.

'He ran right on to one. He wouldn't have—'

I suddenly can't have him speak one more word so I choke out, 'OK. Let's move.'

'It was fast, it happened all at once,' Cillian says.

I'm grateful to him for saying that.

We walk on, quickly, Cillian a few steps ahead of me.

'How do they make them? The minefields?' I ask.

'They don't.' His voice has got loud again. 'There were some left from before. We just use them now to help keep the city clear of skrake. They've set down a load, all around the city from the outskirts in. Some places are worse than others. The road is one of the heaviest set places. You've to know where to put your feet when you get through.'

'You got through.' Cillian says nothing to that. 'What's the city like?'

He stays quiet, and after a minute I look over at him, and he looks at me, right in the eyes. 'It's so good to be out,' he says. 'I never thought I'd see anything else. If they catch us . . . Come *on*.'

It's ahead of us now, I see: the fork in the road, and there, right there, will be the bushes where I left Maeve face-down, discarded.

The sun is going down and Cillian is moving so quickly now he's nearly running. I'm keeping up, just about, but the truth of course is that I don't really want to get to where we're going.

'Did you hear that?' Cillian stops suddenly. His hands are by his sides and his fingers splay out with tension: he is totally still while he listens. I've cocked my head to the side but I can't hear anything. He breaks into a jog before I can respond. He runs noisily, too noisily – anything could hear us coming. Still, I say nothing. He's frightened enough already. I jog along behind him and once again try to keep my brain from getting too far ahead of my feet.

'You saw her, you saw Maeve.' They left her there and took the barrow to take me away from her. My chest is tight and something heavy feels like it wants to scratch its way out of it.

'We're here,' Cillian says. 'I think.'

I glance at him and see that he's sweating and winded. His long, thin arms rise and fall with every breath he takes. I want to ask him if he's all right, but I say instead, quietly, 'Show me.'

Cillian points to a bush and begins to walk towards it.

'This is where we . . . where we found the barrow.'

He hunkers down on all fours and pulls back some branches. I keep moving. I step forwards slowly and kneel beside him. Everything feels as if it's happening very slowly, but I can't stop it. I can't look at the spot where she lies, I cannot.

'Look,' Cillian says. 'That's where the barrow was tipped over, and you can see the—'

I can't hear the rest of his sentence for the blood rushing in my head. I have looked up and yes, I can see where the earth has been disturbed. A thick line for the wheel and two indents for where the barrow was put down fast and then some mess from when it tipped over.

Here we were, the three of us, together, not even a day ago.

The *loss* of it.

There is no body.

'Where is she?' I choke out.

There's a noise, suddenly, a crackle of undergrowth in the bushes, coming from behind us. I feel Cillian tense beside me.

'What is that?' His whisper is terrified.

'Where is she?' I say again.

Cillian says nothing: I turn to look at him but he's his back turned, to look where the noise came from. 'What is that?'

'Cillian,' I say, louder. 'Where did she go?'

'We have to get out of here,' Cillian whispers, and already he's getting up.

'No,' I say, '*no*.'

I crawl deeper into the brush, towards the space where Maeve last lay.

'Come on,' Cillian says, too loudly, and he tries to grab my arm but I shake him off and scrabble forwards, my breath loud in the dark of the undergrowth. There must be a sign, a track, *something*. I'm half aware of noises coming from behind me, a scruffling, but I keep going, elbows digging into the earth, branches scratching at my face. My knives push uncomfortably against my thigh and upper hip. I search desperately; I'm not sure for what.

A touch of her hand on mine.

I hear Cillian cry out in fright, as if from a long way off. Something, it must be him, grabs my ankle and pulls me hard, but I shake him away from me, push forwards again. Cillian is shouting from behind me, I can hear him now, and I know, I *know* I have to go back to him, but then the sun breaks through the clouds and all in a flash I see the way ahead of me. Through the undergrowth, past this bush and not quite into the next, there's a track . . . something rolled away here, down the incline, into the thicker bush and off towards the thicker forest.

'Ah!' Cillian's cry sounds like he's in pain and, cursing, I turn. I back my way quickly through the undergrowth towards the road, over whatever tracks there might be beneath me, ruining them.

I emerge arse-first back into the light of the road's clearing and blink into the sunlight. Cillian is on the ground, on his back, feet and hands flailing wildly in the air, the skrake all over him.

Chapter Twenty-Two

THIS IS WHAT HAPPENED MAM.

A figure in the distance. It catches the scent of her on the wind. Out there somewhere, out in the battleground of Ireland; Mam and Maeve looking around, making sure things were quiet. Imagining me with them, the next time, thinking about what they'll show me and teach me. The skrake scents them both or sees them and starts coming, awkward and fast. Too fast. I try to call up an image of the two of them in which they are not ready, and I cannot.

Still and all, the skrake gets on Maeve, and then Mam has to get between them.

I wonder if there's that sudden connection between them, Mam and the skrake, like fire, like the moment my knife leaves my hand to bring down a gull. Mam would know it, this feeling. She'd know she was caught, and then she would have thought of me, and that hurts to think about. That hurts a lot.

Or, maybe it was different, quicker. Maeve was off getting firewood and she never saw it, maybe. She stumbles and it grabs her and goes for the first thing it can get its mouth to. And Mam comes between them, in the nick of time. It bites hard just as Maeve's knife comes down on its skull. Just a fraction too late. A blink earlier and she'd a been home with a lesson on it, and telling Maeve to keep quiet and not be scaring the child with a story of near-miss.

That fraction of time is why we train, Maeve'd say. And still she was too late.

Mam'd know when it bit her, though; she'd know everything then about what would happen.

Maybe that's why when I hear Maeve shouting furiously up to me from down the road my first feeling is anger. As soon as she cries out to me I know what has happened, and I feel rage for a pure moment before the grief comes.

Maeve has my mother in the barrow we'd left at the little jetty. She is going quickly despite that. I meet her a hundred metres from the house but she barely glances at me.

'Oh, Mam,' I say, when I see her body in the barrow,

146

her eyes closed and head thrown back. There's a smear of something dried on her cheek and her hair is caked with mud but her expression is calm and gentle; her eyes closed, her eyebrows raised just a little. Her head is banging off the barrow with light thuds but Maeve doesn't notice.

I'm crying loudly, sobbing. 'Maeve. *Maeve*.'

She hasn't slept, she is thinner even than a few days ago. That strength she carries around with her like an extra skin is gone; it has been flayed off her.

She doesn't stop so I move with them.

'*Maeve*,' I bawl.

'Whisht,' Maeve tells me.

I try not to look at the body of my mother. One side of her is covered in blood from shoulder to hip. Maeve forces the barrow along broken tarmac, then through weeds and long grass.

'Get in the house,' she tells me, wincing as she stands. I climb up through the bathroom window and turn round to watch Maeve sit my mother up in the barrow, drape her over her shoulder, and then stand. Her legs shake and for a moment I think she won't make it but then she's up, and she turns towards me and tells me to take my mother's hands and pull her in while Maeve pushes. I am delicate at first, afraid to touch Mam's hot, livid skin, but Maeve shouts at me again and her hoarseness pinches through my fear, and I grab on and pull. My mother comes through the window and we both fall, hard. She lands on top of me and I am pinned by her dead weight to the tiny bathroom's floor, my head jammed awkwardly against the wall. The breath is knocked out of me and I try to inhale and can't. I gasp, rasping, breathing in the scent of my mother, which is not like herbs any more but something rotting.

'Maeve.'

I can't get the cry out but then she's there, she's getting through the window with her steady old grace and she lifts my mother off me and I let out a great heaving sob before I can even try to grab hold of it, and I nearly expect a clout around the ear but instead Maeve pulls me to her and holds me tight.

Chapter Twenty-Three

I LAUNCH MYSELF TOWARDS THEM, HANDS FLYING, RAGE sparking.

I get the palm of my hand to its face and push and feel beneath my skin its teeth knock together hard. I'm on its back, and we fall forwards together on top of Cillian, pinning him down against the road, the small weight of me and the bigger weight of the skrake crushing him. I manoeuvre an arm till it's tight around its neck and I pull viciously. I need my other arm to keep it tight and in place but I can't reach for my knives this way and I can't get it off him.

I try to get my knees into its back so I can pull harder, I want to pull its head off its mouldering skrake shoulders.

It flails backwards with its arms, trying to dislodge me. We're free of Cillian. He's on the ground now, lying still, and in the back of my mind somewhere this is worrying, but I've my hands full.

The skrake has me caught by the hair and it pulls hard. I grit my teeth against the pain and hold on tight. There's a tearing, wrenching sensation and it feels like the skrake has taken off a good portion of my scalp, but it's off-balance, and using my feet I propel myself away from it. I land, and I roll awkwardly but stand well (*Maeve, did you see?*), my hands going to my knives as the skrake turns to face me, losing interest now in Cillian's crumpled form on the ground.

It is, it's her, of course it is.

It's Maeve.

My heart within me withers and dies.

She's so changed from what she was: wirier, stronger than ever, covered nearly head to toe in muck. It's on her face and in her hair, her clothes are caked in it. Yesterday's rain, she'd have been out in it. She could have caught her death, my brain prattles stupidly.

Maeve, Maeve.

I'm on my knees on the ground, looking helplessly at her and as I do her eyes flicker and come to life; the haziness over them is blinked away.

'Orpen,' the skrake says.

My mouth opens and closes, and I've decided I've nothing to say to her till I hear the words coming out of my mouth.

'What were you at?'

'Orpen.' Her voice is cracking.

'What were you at that Mam had to get between ye? You were a *team*.'

I get to my feet and feel my own power course through me, the rage. I use it.

On the ground, I can see Cillian moving.

'Orp—'

She doesn't finish getting my name out, her voice plaintive and wheedling and utterly unlike her, before she comes at me. I don't have the time or space to throw, so I swing my leg in a good solid arc for a roundhouse, the power of my anger bubbling up through my hips, crackling in my fingertips, gathering in the muscles of my legs. The bridge of my foot sinks into the hollow beneath Maeve's cheek just so, and I swing on through and she stumbles off to the right under the weight of my strike.

I take two steps back so I can bring a knife level with my ear and it's gone, flying through the air and it lands straight and nearly up to the hilt in Maeve's neck. She lets out a noise, a cry that is somewhere between scream and gurgle, and falls forwards, landing on her hands. Maeve's eyes, though, her eyes never leave me.

She comes for me again, screaming, legs pushing off hard against the ground. I let fly another but it's too late, she's on top of me, pinning me down and snapping at my throat. One hand is on my shoulder, claws digging hard into my flesh, and the other is on my head. I've one arm free, just about, and I reach for another knife, my last: it's further down than the others and though I can touch the hilt with my fingers I can't quite grasp it. Another moment and Maeve will bite into my head and there'll be an end to it, but I shift my hips a little and my fingers just about grab on to the knife and then *THWACK*, her head is thrown to one side.

Cillian is standing above us, a branch of wood in his hand, and he raises it again. I get a glimpse at his terrified face before Maeve gets to her feet to bring back one arm in an arc and fling it through him in a powerful sweep that's nearly graceful. Cillian is too slow to duck, too ignorant to block, and she gets him the full force in the face. He doesn't even let out a cry. There is a dull, damp noise where her fist makes contact and a flash of blood before Cillian falls.

She's on me again before he hits the ground but I've my knife. Her teeth are gnashing wildly and she's so close now it's easier to believe she's just a skrake. My third knife sinks slowly upwards into the soft part of her neck under the jaw. Maeve cries again, and as she opens her mouth wide, blood gushes out.

I can feel her body tense and twitch above me and there's more blood now, hot and rancid, flowing on to my face. I turn my head aside but push the knife deeper upwards into the head. She spasms hard and gurgles again – I feel her teeth snap by my ear – but when she lurches forwards the knife only goes deeper, and the snapping becomes slow and sullen. The knife is all the way in and I begin to work it from side to side, doing as much damage as I can to whatever the blade can reach. I pull it out a little and there is a hiss of foul air, and I work it back in, the handle slippery in my fingers. The knife hesitates against a rubberiness and I pull harder against it and feel something give, and warm black ooze runs down my fingers. It's not till I shove the knife up hard into her ear, or what's left of her ear, that she stops struggling at last.

I nearly don't want to move out from under the weight of her, but I do, wriggling little by little till I can get my arms out and then dragging myself away. I rest with my forearms flat against the ground, breathing deep and spitting. I hope that I will be sick, but there's nothing left in my stomach, only bile. I feel nothing.

When I can move again I crawl to where Cillian lies prone. It is hard to see him in the near-dark but he is breathing, in snuffling, uncomfortable starts. I shake him and for long moments the numbness in me gives way to fresh fear, but then his voice sounds, a whisper in the gloom:

'That was your Maeve, I'd say.'

Though I can feel the dirt under my nails and the itchiness of the blood and bile drying on my skin, the cooling air and the wind rustling the trees, I'm not there. My eyes are streaming. A part of my brain goes on back to Slanbeg and is there in the quietness of the island, and I stay with that. I stay there listening for the noises of Mam and Maeve.

There's a voice I slowly become aware of but it's hard to tune in on and I don't bother. I'd rather stay here on the ground, half in Ireland and half away, and numb. I turn my head away from Cillian and let the tears keep streaming and close my eyes. I'm not here, I could nearly say to him. I'm gone now. Let time go on and pass without me, I've no interest in it.

Cillian is doing something: moving, calling me. I turn my head and close my eyes against him but he touches my hand and the feel of skin against skin turns something in me and I fright away, crying out, thinking it's something else, something new coming to get me. My thoughts make no sense to myself.

'Orpen,' Cillian whispers, and he has his hands up as if he thinks I'll attack him. 'Orpen, listen,' and there's no other noise so I can't help hearing it then. Movements. Skrake moving through the undergrowth. Humans wouldn't move like that. There's more than one.

Good, I think viciously to myself.

'We have to move,' Cillian whispers. He reaches a hand out for me but I flinch away and wrap my arms around my knees and put my head on to them. I'm going nowhere.

'Come on!' Cillian hisses, putting his hands on top of mine and pulling them towards him, but I dig in. The shuffling sounds are getting louder, nearer.

'Just go,' I say. 'Just go, I'll be OK, just go.'

I don't know what I'm saying.

Maeve is dead.

Cillian lets go of my hands, backs away slowly, his eyes full of terror, of near-panic. I recognise it, numbly, from far away. He looks over his shoulder, westwards. 'Just go, just go,' I'm saying, and I'm not sure if I'm saying it out loud or not. Cillian turns, runs a few steps, looks back again. His face is so full of fear.

I let myself sit down and I take a big breath. It'll be OK. Staying is easier.

Cillian is at Maeve's body, gathering up my knives and wiping the blades hastily on his trousers. I watch through a film of tears, beaten. He hunkers beside me, and he puts his hands on my face and I flinch away again but he doesn't move off.

'She's gone! She's dead!' He's saying the words right into my face, looking into my eyes with his. It's too intense, it's such an invasion, I could punch him. 'You know she's dead,' he's saying, none too quietly. 'She was dead the moment she got bitten. You set her free, Orpen. She's free, she's gone now.'

I blink slowly at him. Tears have made a track through the dirt on his face. His red lips and green eyes stand out against the grime – he looks wildly around us, expecting the skrake to be on him any moment. He is beautiful, I think dimly, without interest. My hands have found my knives on the ground beside us and I pick them up, one by one, thoughtlessly. Cillian is speaking again and I try to follow what he's saying.

'Would she want you to stay? Would she want you to die here?'

There's a sudden noise behind us, a snap and then the sound of teeth gnashing, and I flinch away from the noise and get to my feet without meaning to at all. Cillian has hold of me then and he's dragging me and I'm up. We run together.

Chapter Twenty-Four

WE GET MY MOTHER TO HER ROOM. IT IS ARDUOUS AND it's not dignified, but Maeve gets her on to the bed and I wash some of the muck off and smooth back her hair from her face and hold her hand.

I can feel the tiredness come off Maeve in waves, but she doesn't stop moving till she gets things done. I'm helpless. I can do nothing but blink back tears and shock and try to make Mam look more comfortable.

As if that matters.

Mam. Oh, Mammy.

I try not to think, which is easy enough. Thinking in a straight line won't be easy again for a long time.

Maeve shows me the wound. It doesn't even look like a

bite; it's worse than a bite. It's on her left side, a mouthful, big and toothy, taken out of her soft flesh. A part of my mother's own self torn violently away from her. I try to imagine how much it must have hurt, the sheer brutal pain, and cannot. The violence of it is shocking to me, despite everything I've been taught.

'It's not bleeding,' I say. I hear the stupid hope in my voice.

'Clean it,' Maeve tells me, her voice flat as she moves up towards the head of the bed. I watch as she takes my mother's wrist, and I think she is going to feel for her pulse but instead she takes twine from her pocket and she ties one end around Mam's hand and the other to the bed. She pulls the knots tight. There's no gentleness in the movement. It reminds me of something.

'I don't know how,' I say. I sound small and far away.

'You do. I've told you.' Maeve has moved around to the other side of the bed and once she's finished there she leaves the room. I hear her going into her bedroom, and then water sloshing around in her basin, water that has been there since I bought it up to her the morning she and Mam left. Days and days ago.

The sound of my breathing is loud in the room. I can't take my eyes off my mother's calm, closed face. Her chest rises and falls slowly, nearly imperceptibly. We inhale at the same moment, my mother's lungs and my own.

I shiver.

I know now what Maeve's matter-of-fact motions with the string reminded me of. She looked just the way she does when she's getting a chicken ready for the fire.

My mother's wound is too big to be closed so I can only clean it, which Maeve knew already.

I wince as I try to wash the hole in her side in boiled water, expecting her to flinch, to cry out. There's a lot of wound and not enough skin to cover it. I wash the blood away and look closely at the red flesh: it makes me feel nauseous and itchy, looking at it. The edges of the wound are turning black and green. It looks infected. I wonder what we're going to give her, how she's going to recover from this. I wonder even as I know there'll be no recovery.

I haven't worked out why Maeve brought Mam home yet.

Instead of thinking too hard, I go out to the chickens, and I feed them and collect eggs and I check the fence and I weed the vegetables and pull potatoes, and I draw water and then more water and lug it back to the house, and then I'm still so tired I can't close my eyes without seeing my mother's festering bite, so I drill myself on techniques and then I run the course. Moving is only just marginally better than not moving.

I don't sleep much but I don't get up, I'm too afraid of the day, till Maeve bangs on my door.

Training doesn't stop, not even for death. I was told this before but I suppose I didn't believe it. There were a whole load of things I was taught that I didn't believe.

'Come back to the house after morning chores,' Maeve calls in to me and later, when I'm back, she is waiting for me in the kitchen, our war council room.

Her face looks much older than it did a week ago, before they set off. She looks as if she has been grabbed and shaken roughly, spun around and pushed off in a direction she doesn't want to go. A game we used to play on birthdays when I was a child.

'Are you OK?' I ask her.

She looks at me as if I've just taken a load of chicken-shit and rubbed it over my face.

'This is what's going to happen now,' she tells me after a pause. Her voice is gruffer even than usual, as if she's coming down with a cold. I wonder how much rest she's had. 'We'll document any changes. We'll learn. We'll watch till it wakes. And then you'll kill it.'

It takes me long moments to catch up with what she's saying, with what she means by 'it'. I can't breathe: it feels like something has landed on top of me. Dizzily, I put my hands to my head.

'No,' I say, 'I won't.'

'You will.' It's the way Maeve says it – there's no doubt in there; she has all the second guesses that the sea does, or a storm. She sounds how she always sounds. But we're standing in the kitchen talking about me killing my mother.

'You can't make me.' I believe her already, though, that I'll do it. I'm too shocked to cry but she'll get me to do this, one way or the other. 'I'll leave.'

'Yes, you may leave, if you must,' Maeve says, and has a long drink from her mug.

She knows I won't go anywhere. She knows that I know I'll die out there without her.

'I'll go to the mainland,' I tell her, surprising myself. 'I'll find Phoenix City. I'll find a cure.'

Maeve's expression changes at last. She's angry, now, furious, and in one movement she gets to her feet and throws her mug at the wall beside me; it smashes, and little drops of steaming water scald me, the wall, the floor. I cry out but Maeve hasn't even paused, she is shouting.

'What do you know about it, what do you know about Phoenix City?' Her hands are bunched into fists and I'm on my feet, in my guard, but quivering, devastated with fright.

'I've seen it written,' I say. 'Why did you teach me to read if I wasn't to learn? It's on papers, they say to go there and you'll be safe.'

A moment passes and Maeve runs her hands through

her dirty hair, making it stick up. She looks away, through the cracks in the planks over the window.

'Don't mention that place to me again, do you hear me?' she says, quieter. 'That city is long dead.'

'But it existed?' I whisper, still shaking, not relaxing my guard.

'It used to.'

'It's not on any maps,' I tell her.

She stares at me, furious.

'Why do you never tell me anything?'

She turns round again to look at me: she looks me right in the eyes.

'Phoenix City was in the east,' she says, hard and fast and final. 'It wasn't a good place and it's gone now. Those things you read, what they say isn't true any more. If it ever was.'

'So we're to stay here, just Mam and yourself and me, for ever?'

'What do you think we've been doing, putting our lives in danger every time we leave the island? We've been looking for – for more for you.' She's still angry but she's trying, trying to tell me the things she thinks I need to know and her words about how they'd been off searching, despite the danger, knowing what might happen, they hit hard, so they do. I thought they were leaving to test me, or punish me. Or just to be away. So I did.

Maeve looks so tired. She seems small for the first time in my life. She puts a hand to her forehead and takes one breath, in and out slowly, and there's a catch to her voice when she speaks again.

'Your mother is dead, love.'

Only Mam calls me that, calls me love. Hearing that word in her mouth makes me so angry.

'She was dead the moment she was bitten, you know that. That's what we've been teaching you, all along.'

'You do it, then,' I tell her. 'You can do it.' I find it hard to get the words out. I cannot get myself in control.

Maeve nods. It's a brisk nod.

'It's a skrake, it's not your mother. If I end it now, it will be over, but you'll have learnt nothing. We have to use everything we have, everything. When the skrake is conscious and moving and hungry, you'll end it. I'll help you.'

She stops talking, waiting for my sobs to subside, but minutes pass and they don't. Eventually, she moves from her seat towards me and I flinch and take my hands from my face, but Maeve pulls me to her and holds me tight to her again.

'She saved me,' Maeve says quietly. 'It had me and she got in its way. She'd never've been bitten otherwise, only saving me. She got bitten so I could come home to you.'

I shudder into Maeve's warm, strong shoulder.

'She wanted me to get back to you so that we could keep training, so I could keep making you strong.' She pulls away, and takes my face in her hands and looks so deep, so unflinchingly, into me that I can't even blink.

Chapter Twenty-Five

I'M BREATHING HARD BUT CILLIAN IS WORSE. I LET GO HIS hand and keep a pace or two behind him so there's something between his body and whatever's chasing us. He's not moving fast enough. I'm operating on something pure, on instinct or reflex.

Training, Maeve says somewhere within me, and the numbness I feel goes a little deeper, claws on to me a little harder.

We keep going, up an incline and I keep my hands on his back, pushing him. I've bruises, hard bruises, but I'm not in much physical pain and Cillian is, I think. If I'd to guess I'd say his nose is broken and there could be more besides. There's not a bit I can do about that, and it'll be the absolute least of our problems if we don't keep well ahead of the skrake, so I keep quiet and follow after him, listening behind us.

Up ahead, Cillian stumbles and I feel pity for him, and something like admiration, except it's so different from the feelings I'd have had for Maeve and Mam. He's working so hard, I think, because he's running towards Nic, and Aodh. He trips and falls in front of me, and I scoop him upwards as we go, catching him beneath the arms and yanking. He's already picking himself up, rubbing the palms of his hands together. His reddish hair is dark with sweat around the temples, and his face is a mess of dried blood and swollen skin. I take a look over my shoulder at the road behind us. I can't see anything.

I move a little ahead of him, making him keep up with me now. And we keep going. My throat is dry and I realise I'm parched. Cillian is worse, probably. I remember the yoke he has strapped around his body and I reach for it and tug it off him, hold on to him to let him know we'll rest, let him catch his breath. I find the stopper and bring it to his lips. He drinks a little, coughs, and then takes more, long sucking draughts that have him breathing even harder. He sits down on the ground, panting.

'I'm OK,' he mumbles through snot, phlegm and water while I take my turn with his bottle. Three mouthfuls, I decide. That's my allowance. The water is cool and crisp-tasting. Cillian bends over, puts his hands on his thighs and spits on to the dust.

'I'll be OK,' he says again, and he looks up to meet my eyes. 'Are you?'

I can't hear anything following us; probably we're safe enough, but I don't feel it. *You're never safe, ever.*

'C'mon,' I say. 'A little further.'

I don't think he'll be able, but Cillian gets going again: he stands straight, takes a step, wobbles. I jump to my feet and he puts a hand to my shoulder. He steadies himself. He takes a deep breath, spits again, takes another, and then starts moving again. I pick up the wraparound water bottle and I follow.

We move on, more slowly now, as the light goes and the landscape around us darkens. We break often and drink small sips, but ages later we're still going. At last we walk side by side and I swing Cillian's empty water bottle by its long sling. I haven't seen or heard a skrake since a little after we left the crossroads before the minefield. Still we walk.

The day is disappearing on us. After a long trudge uphill, we get to the top of a slope and stop again for a break. I hunker down to stretch and feel my knees pop and my feet throb. We've a good view of the road ahead of us, miles outwards to the west. West, I think, homewards. The sun is setting, throwing a rosy glow over the whole of Ireland, it feels like. It's so beautiful.

And that way, over there, is Slanbeg, still the same, but gone for ever.

Cillian shields his bloodied face with his hand, his eyes searching the landscape below us. 'I can't see anything,' he tells me, his voice cracked with exhaustion.

He's looking for Aodh and Nic, of course. The skrake are left behind us I'd say, but I want to move still.

'Another while,' I say. 'I see a place we can get water.' Besides this, I don't like being on top of a hill; we've a good view but we're exposed and we're too bone-tired to take on a gust of wind just now.

Cillian follows me without argument. For maybe three klicks I listen to his dragging feet following me. We get to the place I saw on the hill and I lead him off-road, through the growth till we find the river. Cillian half sits, half falls on to its bank and I'm the same, dog-tired, spent. Our breathing starts to even out, and the quiet around us gets louder. I don't think at all about Maeve.

Technically, I should keep watch, but when night fills out we're both fast asleep, spread out beside the river.

Cillian's still out when I wake up, but he must have stirred in the night: my body is close to his, near touching, and though the ground is freezing beneath me, sapping the warmth from my body, there are blankets over us both. He must have woken in the cold and got them from his pack.

Delicately, not moving too much, I take inventory. I'm refreshed, give or take, and the aches in my shoulder and bruises along my thighs and the sides of my face feel no worse than the bruises I'd get from training. I'm fine, nothing a few days of rest won't cure for good. The numbness is lifting. I feel as if my body belongs to myself, as if it's something I'm connected to.

Maeve.

I won't think about it, is all. If I think about it, I'll stop again, I'll lie myself down on the ground and Cillian won't be able to get me moving this time.

He is sleeping hard beside me, as if he has nothing to be afraid of. His arms are curled up beside his bloodied face and I can see the clean delicate skin of his inner wrist, the shadows his long eyelashes cast on his face. It feels good to lie beside him, but when I close my eyes to rest more, I see Maeve's face, bloodied, turned, her lips forming an 'O'. I get moving, up and out of the little patch of warmth I'd made on the ground for the night and away from thought and memory and into the safety of exercise.

I stretch in the cold air, but before I settle into my morning routine I steal back through the bushes to see if there's anything worth seeing on the road. It's clear in every direction.

I'm thinking now.

I throw water from the little stream on my face and I

drink and rinse out my mouth and my cuts and scrapes, and then it's down to work, down to training. I keep an eye on Cillian and the world around us. I go easy on myself – I'm still sore – but it's good to be doing it, good to be moving again. It warms me up and makes me feel loose and ready. Maeve would be satisfied with me, a thought comes, and I clamp down my mind on it like a lid on a box.

No thinking.

I work harder.

When I'm finished I drink from and then refill the water-bag and then go waking Cillian. He's in deep and it takes him a while to come to. He coughs, raises himself on an elbow. I hand him the water and get going, moving slowly so he can catch up when he's ready. I hear him behind me, big feet noisy and unpractised on the road.

After a while he asks, 'How long was I sleeping?'

'All of the night and part of the day,' I say, my voice coming out annoyed-sounding.

'You should have woken me sooner.'

'It's not up to me to be waking you,' I tell him, before I can stop myself, and he's quiet after that.

I have to try harder. I don't know why I'm so like her. My mind flinches away from her name.

When the sun's high we break to drink water. My stomach gives a rumble and I let out a little laugh that sounds like an apology. Cillian acknowledges it with a huffing sort of noise and reaches for his pack.

'I should have done this this morning, or yesterday even,' he says. 'It was hard to think.'

In his hand he has a tin: he screws off the top and inside is a wobbling, greasy-looking substance. He puts a hand in it and then reaches for me. I start, hand going reflexively to a knife.

'It's cream,' he says. His voice is soothing but he sounds like I hurt him. 'Like Nic used. It'll help with your cuts.'

'Moving towards me quickly can be dangerous,' I say by way of explanation, but he doesn't look like he understands what I mean and I don't know how to say it any clearer.

'Look,' he says, and dabs some on his nose. He winces with the pain of it but keeps going, rubbing it on the swollen bridge of his nose and around his nostrils. It's not pleasant to watch. The last of the caked blood starts to come away and he's wincing and letting out air between his teeth. After a moment, though, he's dabbing more vigorously. 'It helps with the pain. It disinfects as well. Come here.'

I move forwards a little, more curious than anything else. I perch warily while he applies the ointment to the side of my face. His touch is gentle; I close my eyes for a moment and I realise that all the little hairs on my arms and neck and even my thighs are standing upwards. I stand up abruptly and walk away a little, pretend to stretch.

'It'll start to feel better soon,' Cillian says quietly, behind me. I hear him digging around in his bag, opening and closing things. 'There's water near here?'

I point to the place, on just twenty paces from us, and let him go alone while I drop down for another few press-ups. I listen hard in case there's trouble.

Cillian comes back, fiddling with small brown pellets and a plastic container. He adds some water to the pellets and tells me, 'It'll be edible soon. Then we'll move.' He looks up at me, catching my eyes with his. 'Are you OK?' he asks. 'Yester—'

'Don't,' I tell him, my voice like a stone.

He nods. I wish he wouldn't watch me.

'Don't stare,' I say. I want to tell him somehow to keep his eyes off my face: it's too personal, whatever he sees there. I don't want to be looked at, especially not in the eyes.

'OK.'

We look at the landscape around us while the food readies itself. The green of the grass is particularly violent-looking against the darkening sky. It is beautiful.

Cillian speaks again after a little while. I know he will. 'What's it like, where you come from?'

He hands me the tin. I take it in my hands and am surprised to feel that it's warm. Cillian digs into his bag again and finds me a spoon. I dig in. The food is rich and good and hot. Six small mouthfuls, I think. And the rest for him. Cillian watches me while I eat, and when I hand the dish over to him he licks the spoon clean and nods to himself and says, 'What do you do for food? How safe is it there?'

It's good, nearly, to have him asking this again. He's scared but he's all right. In my mind's eye I call up Slanbeg. I keep my thoughts away from our house (Mam's hat hanging in the hall, waiting for her, Maeve's winter jumper, folded carefully). I try to imagine that the rest of the chickens might have survived this long.

What happens when we catch up to Nic and Aodh? They'll be with Cillian. I'm just someone that tried to force them all into more danger. To try to get a look at a body that had already turned, and then nearly had both of us ate.

And I was mean about it.

Even so, I tell the truth. 'Nowhere's safe.'

Chapter Twenty-Six

I SIT BY MAM'S BED AND WATCH HER FINISH DYING AND THIS is my training now.

I pace, I shadow-box, I get through double and triple helpings of press-ups on the floor in her room. I read while I wait for her to wake up and devour me.

I think about the symptoms, the ones Maeve knows for sure and the ones she doesn't. I remember everything: the whole story from sorry beginning to messy, bloody end. I know as much as anyone probably knows, so I do, and it's still not enough.

You might think that the bodily functions of a person who has been bitten would have the decency to quit, but they do not. Early on Maeve tells me to go looking for all the sheets I can find in the village. I wash the worst of the dust and filth off them, dry them, and after they've been used we throw them out one by one. We've never wasted anything but there's no good in trying to wash these. Maeve and I change my mother, her body, the best we can, but once the mattress gets it, there's only so much we can do.

The smell is awful, more pungent than death, more active. The window is open and the breeze is good, but in the day sweat rolls off me and at night I freeze. Maeve takes over for six hours every night to let me sleep, and then I'm back with her at sunrise.

The house is quiet with dread. I am frightened and also bored, and ashamed for being bored. Maeve isn't often in the room with me, only when she's the chores of three people all done, but she doesn't go further than shouting distance from the house now. The chickens are brought in, the far garden is mostly untended. She sits with me in silence, and though I breathe easier when she's there, I hate us being in the same room. The anger courses through me like my own blood and I hold it as close. She was always hard with me, Maeve, but I'm hard back to her now. I hate her and blame her and that makes me feel a little better.

On the fifth day Mam throws up black bile, without ever waking up. The vomit pours from her lips and bubbles in her throat and comes out her nostrils. I jump up, shaking, and shout for Maeve. When she comes, she shifts my mother on to her side, and more vomit comes up. We clean up. The gurgling, bubbling noises stop eventually.

On the seventh day, the seizures start. At first they're only small episodes of twitching, but then they get worse. I count, my own body shaking, while my mother flails uncontrollably, violently on the bed. Out of everything, these are the worst.

The strings on her wrists and feet dig into the skin so that it bleeds and once she's quieted down again I pick them out of the flesh, wincing while my mother lies unconscious.

I go a bit mad, I think, watching this. Lots of things die in that room: half my life.

Maeve sits with me.

'It's about respect as well,' she says, as if we'd been in the middle of a conversation and I hadn't been paying attention.

I say nothing and it takes her a while to go on, to get at what she's really trying to tell me. She used silence on me all the time I was growing up and now I want to use it back on her. I want to use any weapon I can get against her.

'It's about making this part as easy and as dignified as you can for her.'

'It's not her,' I say, wondering does it hurt her. My voice sounds strange in my ears, older. 'It's a shell. She's dead.' I take a breath and then say the thing I've been working up to. 'Where were you, Maeve? What were you at that she got bitten?'

The quiet in the room is like a kick in the stomach but I will not break it. She's nothing to say to that and I feel like I've got something back. I steal a glance over towards her and I have to look again, and then again. She is crying, silently.

'Good girl,' she says after a moment, making no effort to wipe at her eyes.

What a poor swap I am for my mother.

'Would you rather she was on her own?' Maeve asks. 'Would you rather I had left her there?'

'I'd rather you were there for her,' I say, but I'm thinking about the things Maeve meant me to, despite myself. I think about Mam, or my mother's living corpse, left out under the stars and the heat and the rain on the mainland, shitting herself and puking black mucus, and left to die and then to hunger for ever. I think about her beautiful dark hair clotted with mud and filth, and her damp forehead with nobody to wipe the sweat off it.

My ears and throat and eyes are swollen from crying but I seem to be giving it another go anyway. I shake my head.

Maeve doesn't need to look right at me to know it.

'We should clean her,' I say. 'We should give her a proper clean and wash her hair and put her in new sheets. And then you should.'

I can't say it.

Beside me, Maeve sighs. 'Should what?'

I won't say it.

After a long time, she says, 'And what about what she wanted? You have to respect that as well. Your mother has gone, but there's still value to her death, and if I take my knife and push it through her eye it'll be a betrayal of what she stood up to that pain for. So. Pity about you.'

She ends her sentence sounding cross and hearing a trace of her old familiar anger makes me feel a little better.

'How long does it take?'

'It's different for everyone. Some take five days, some fifteen. Some people wake up sometimes, nearly like themselves, but others don't at all. There's no relying on it.'

'There must be something we can do, there must be someone to help us. How do you know anything, where did you learn—'

'There isn't,' Maeve says, clear and simple, and I don't believe her, and I hate her, I *hate* her. 'There's no one out there can help us.'

We don't talk about it again. We don't talk much about anything again.

The end happens on the morning of the twelfth day.

The stinking sweat she'd had seemed to abate. She hadn't vomited in a long time. It looked for all the world like she might be getting better. I let myself believe it a little. Couldn't some people just get well again?

I take over from Maeve as usual at the end of the night. 'Any changes?'

She doesn't bother respond, only leaves the room.

The house is quiet now, watchful. I scribble in my training journal, look over old notes. I draw in the margins, pictures of buildings and people, and then, restless, I get down on the floor for some stretches.

The hands of the body on the bed are twitching but I'm used to it now.

I didn't do my press-ups yesterday. After five years of getting through them every day, when I was ten and had what Mam called a chest infection and Maeve called lung rot, and every month when I'm crippled with period pain and I couldn't face them, I did them anyway. I thought I'd feel different if I missed them. And I did, I felt worse. Today I'll do double, and maybe that will prove that our little life is not ending, or that if it is, I'm ready for it.

At first I don't hear it, or I think it's a ghost or my imagining. I'm between press-ups and I pause for a moment, my nose almost touching the floor, my arms poised, strong, like they could hold me for ever. I hold my breath, but the room is silent. I get through a few more before I hear it again, and the second time, it's clear.

'Orpen.' My mother's voice.

Her voice is strong.

It sounds just like her.

It scares the shit out of me.

I use my arms to propel me towards the door, my knees coming up protectively, my hands going automatically to a guard position.

'Orpen, love.'

Chapter Twenty-Seven

SOMETIMES I'LL WAKE FROM MY NUMB, HALF-SLEEPING walk and think it's Maeve beside me.

We're getting better at it now, the two of us. We're aware: if one of us is dragging their feet we take a break and drink some water. It's always Cillian but sometimes I'll pretend so he gets a rest before he marches himself into the road.

I try not to feel like I'm going in the wrong direction.

We pick our way through a small town – it doesn't look familiar to me and I worry about that. I wish I'd my map still.

The thunder cracks the sky open and we both jump. On

our left is a small building made out of red bricks and we run into it out of the rain. Inside, the hall is dim, the light soft. We wander quietly. The building is squat and solid-feeling, I've no fear it'll cave in on top of us. It smells musty, and though the rain makes a racket the quiet of being inside the place makes us want to move carefully. My solitude with Cillian feels more intense, gathered in here between walls.

We don't stray far from each other. The floor is littered with dust and rubbish. I'd have loved a building like this on the island. I'd have stayed for hours, rooting around for things to bring home and hide to inspect them later and use as part of the jigsaw I was making to try to put the-world-as-it-was back into one piece.

I follow Cillian into one of the rooms off the main corridor. It's lighter in here, and warm, the glass of the windows still in one piece. There are rows of tiny desks and little seats, and a bigger table at one side. The drawers are open and there are papers everywhere.

'I think it was a school,' he says quietly.

On one wall there are tiny faded handprints in different colours. I go to sit down but my backside is too big to let me comfortably in behind the little wooden desk. There's a board at the head of the classroom on the wall and in the dust on it some long-ago hand wrote 'Help me'.

In a corner there's a large brown stain. The smell is old

and squalid. I sit quiet, listening, my head on my arms, my eyes closed. Imagine going somewhere where you'd have all these people, each entirely different but maybe all of them friends, and there'd be some of them there to teach you whatever you wanted, and there'd be someone to answer whatever question you had about anything. Someone who had to talk to you, to tell you things.

I think about all the kids here that never got a life at all, the kids this school couldn't keep safe. I try to feel lucky.

'Let's make camp here?'

We should wait out the storm and go on again for another few hours, but it is a good place to rest and Cillian probably hasn't the hours left in him.

We find another room, one that's nearly clear of furniture and has a way out off from the building through shrubs if we need it, and after I've checked everything over we make little nests for ourselves to sleep in and we settle down for the night.

I don't say much but Cillian talks to me anyway, his voice soft, and I try to be warmer. When he hands me water I take it from him gratefully and drink deep.

'It's the bag,' he tells me, though I've asked him nothing. 'They used to make them back when. They'd line them with something, minerals or vitamins or I don't know, and they make the water taste good. Cold and clean. You can piss in it even and it'll be OK to drink. After a while.'

I listen intently but say nothing, taking in not so much the words as the voice, the depth of it, and something deep in me answering it.

'It's called a canten, because if you fill it right up it's meant to last one person for ten days . . . These things, they don't last for ever, though. A few years' use and the water doesn't taste so good. They don't have that many of them, in the city, but we took two on our way out, and the pepcho, the fixem and the shtorella. If they caught us . . . I don't know why you'd want to go there.'

'Pepcho. That's the food stuff that goes warm?'

'Yeah. Most people in the city, they don't get that.'

'They make those things in Phoenix City?'

'Not now.'

Like with the bombs, the mines.

Cillian doesn't say more, and I fight the urge to ask him again about the city and settle for watching him closely. He's so tired, and talking is making it worse. He moves funny, different from the way Mam and Maeve would, like he has energy but doesn't know where to put it. He's clumsy.

We sit quietly for a while and I can feel him nearly asleep beside me. I steal looks in the gloom, at the line of his jaw, his thick eyebrows. He twitches a little and, heart jolted, I look away, and watch the walls instead.

I feel like steel beneath the tiredness. That's what Maeve

184

and a lifetime of training have given me. Cillian doesn't have that but he'd keep going, done in as he is. That's what love has given him.

'We'll catch up to them soon,' Cillian says, half asleep.

I don't tell him that I'm surprised we haven't caught them already. We've been walking hard and I'd thought they'd be moving slower, watching for us. For him. I saw no footprints in the mud on the road, in the few hours between heat and wet when tracks can be recorded in the mud. They'd a good start on us and maybe they're walking nearly as fast. It's a worry, and if we don't find them tomorrow, it'll be more like a panic. I don't know how long Cillian will be able to keep calm.

Soon he's breathing evenly, and slowly, carefully, I get closer with my body till I can feel the warmth coming off him.

'Do you think we passed them?'

Cillian is nearly as frightened as he should be. We're sitting at the side of the road, resting again. The sun is high in the sky already.

'In the night? They could have been sleeping at the side of the road.'

'I don't know,' I say honestly. If I knew, I'd be moving faster, less hesitantly.

If he were Maeve these words wouldn't even be

necessary. I'd rather they weren't necessary.

'We should go back,' he says. He starts the sentence firmly but finishes in the end with a question.

I squint my eyes against the sun to look him full in the face, just as he turns to look at me. I look away.

'You always do that,' he says.

'What?'

'You won't look me in the eye.' He sounds angry.

It's true. I find it hard for us both to be looking at each other at the same time. Cillian is still watching me. It's as if he is asking things of me and I don't know how to give them or even if I have them to give. I close my eyes and roll my shoulders.

'Maeve and I didn't. There was no need.' Saying her name is hard and I'm angry now, with him. 'What's the point in it anyway?'

I don't open my eyes to look at him, but I can feel him understand.

'Sorry,' I say, and regret it. Then, briskly, 'Let's get moving.'

'Forwards or back?'

'We've been behind us already.'

There isn't much logic to this but Cillian nods.

'OK,' I say pretending that I'm Maeve and he's me. 'If you want to go back, I'll come with you.' I try to think, to decide. 'My gut's pulling me west,' I find myself saying, and as I say it I see that it is true. Another couple of days west and we'll be near Slanbeg.

'That sounds horrible,' Cillian says. He rubs his hair with one hand and squints at me and my heart gives an uncomfortable thud. His smile is small, half-secret. 'I'm with you.'

It was bad enough knowing I was in charge because I was bullying it out of him. Leading Cillian because he trusts me is worse. I move on, walking faster than I should and making it hard for him to keep up. I want to walk these thoughts right out of myself.

In the afternoon, though, when it starts to lash, we keep on. Every time I look at him now he's more wild-eyed. We walk and face up to getting wet. With each other for warmth in the night I'm not so frightened of the cold and damp.

Thunder rumbles and roars around us and the rain hits the ground so hard that it bounces back up to hit us again. Steam rises from the hot road and the air smells of dirt and freshness. It's delicious.

We won't be able to hear the noise of a skrake over the racket of the storm. Cillian marches on, though, ahead of me now, and I don't try to slow him down. By walking through the rain we leave our prints: our tracks will dry in the sun and be obvious to anyone looking for us till the next time it rains. I hope Nic and Aodh are the only ones trying to find us. I keep an eye out for theirs in the road ahead of us once the rain stops.

Cillian is unhappy, quieter than usual and biting his fingers.

'Would we find their ashes?' I ask. As if the rain wouldn't wash them away. We're resting a few minutes under a rusted metal roof.

Cillian shakes his head. 'I left them the primus.' When I don't respond he says, impatiently, 'It works with a small blue flame. It wouldn't show up in the dark unless you're on top of them. Anyway, they don't need to cook, they have pepcho.' His words are short and hard-sounding.

'Didn't you think about this? Didn't you think about what might happen, if you got separated, how you'd meet up again?'

Suddenly I'm angry – it's popping on my skin and shooting from my fingertips and buzzing from my aching head and bubbling up my throat. The anger feels good, a relief from fear and responsibility. It has been coming for days. 'Where were your Just-In-Cases?'

Without realising it I have got up from my seat in the damp dirt and I let my voice get loud. I want to scream at Cillian till my throat gives way. My hands tighten into fists.

Cillian flinches away from me and then gets up as well, brushing dirt from his hands.

'Maeve and I would have checklists,' I say, still too loud.

I close my eyes against the last of the day's light and try to breathe easier, go quieter. He is struggling. I am struggling. I don't know where that sudden rage came from.

'We called it the JICs list,' I go on, trying to calm down, to get my voice quieter. 'For what we'd do, just in case. If she disappeared one day off the island. Or if I got lost somewhere, or if I met a skrake, or another person. We'd lists for everything, for every Just-In-Case.'

'Has that worked well for you?' Cillian says in a tight, angry voice, and I feel my cheeks get hot with surprise. 'Ha?'

He takes a step towards me and I see how tall he is – he has a good three inches on me. Disguising the move with a casual half-step backwards, never taking my eyes off his, I lower my hand to my knives.

'We tried to save you,' Cillian says. 'I said no, I said to leave you and you were trouble, and fuck was I right, but we *did* save you! And still you dragged me back here – for what? Why the fuck are you shouting at *me*?'

Cillian brings his hands up to his hair again and tugs on it. 'You threaten me and Nic, and Aodh. What were you dragging her out here for in that barrow, your Maeve?' His voice gets quieter now but he's still furious. It's been in there, his anger with me, the whole time. 'Didn't you have a JICs for that, for what to do when she got bit?'

I look away.

189

'You did.' Cillian's voice changes. 'You did, didn't you, and your Maeve wanted one of your knives in her skull? You *stupid*—'

Before I know that I'm going to do it my hand curves upwards and I torque my body round and catch Cillian with a stinging right hook. It lands hard; his nose spurts blood and he staggers back.

'I'm sorry,' I say immediately.

I bite my tongue to stop myself saying more and try to take him by the hand, to sit him down, but he shakes me off. Instead I go looking in his pack for fixem and after a pause he takes it off me, tilting his head back and putting his fingers to the bridge of his nose.

'That's it, isn't it?' he spits at me, his voice nasal and wet-sounding. 'Violence for everything, except for mercy.'

His strike is better than mine. Tears come to my eyes and I look away, stay quiet for a while. Cillian carefully touches his face to see what new damage I did him.

'I'm sorry,' I say again. I put my hands on my head and close my eyes and pace. Right on the most damaged part of his nose; it must have hurt like hell. My knuckles sting pleasantly and I rub them against my thigh.

'She would have wanted you to live,' Cillian says after a bit. He's still pinching the bridge of his nose but he's looking at me out of the sides of his eyes. 'You had a good life, somewhere, both of you?'

I nod, and meet his eye. 'We did.'

'Just you and nobody else?'

'Just us.'

'Where?' His voice urgent.

'Further west, off the end of this road. There's an island.'

'And there's no skrake there?'

'I'll show you,' I tell him.

Chapter Twenty-Eight

'O RPEN?'

I don't breathe.

Mam raises herself till she can rest on her elbows and look at me. I am across the room, frozen, staring at her. I swallow.

'Mam?'

'Love.' My mother's eyes are wincing against the half-light in the room. She looks around, confused, and then looks at me and tries to smile through cracked lips. 'How's my warrior?'

I am crying. I should call for Maeve but instead I say, 'How do you feel?'

'I have the worst headache.' She grimaces and swallows

thickly. 'Be a good girl, get your mam a drink of water,' she says, her voice breaking, looking at the jug and glass beside me.

She hasn't noticed the strings around her wrists and ankles and I don't want her to, I know how that would upset her. I stand up out of my chair and I put my hand to the jug, fill up a glass with warm water.

'I was having awful dreams,' Mam whispers.

She sounds so sad.

She sounds all right, though, nearly.

'It's OK,' I turn to say to her. 'You're OK now.'

'Orpen,' she says. 'What happened?'

'You're home,' I say. 'You're safe.'

'Orpen, come here. Come here to me.' My mother lifts a hand to reach out but it's caught suddenly by the twine. Her hand snaps back. She moves her other hand, her feet. 'Orpen?'

'Mam,' I say, 'it's OK. Everything's OK.' I can barely get the words out through my teeth.

I wonder as I put the water down next to her will she go for me. Will the skrake in her try now to get me?

I don't care too terribly. I just want to feel her arms around me.

'My child,' my mother says.

I reach for her and she reaches for me.

'Baby,' she says once more, and she smiles, and I see her teeth, smell her dead breath.

Those teeth. I don't want those teeth on me.

I pull back just as her jaws crash together: I feel them in my ear, feel the warm breath of exhalation just at my neck. I step back, away from the bed, trip over my own feet and land hard on my arse. I try to push myself back towards the wall with my feet but they keep slipping on the floor. I can't get them to grip.

My mother is not my mother.

She bites the air wildly, her eyes mad. She pulls against her restraints, the muscles and tendons in her neck standing out. I take it all in. I watch her – it – as I try to get away and cannot. Everything happens in seconds, and lasts an age.

My bare heels dig into the floor at least, and I push myself away from the thrashing thing on the bed till my back hits the wall, but it isn't far enough, not by some way. I'm breathing hard and I can't think, I can't even scream. She's still coming, pulling everything she's got towards me. Her hair is in her face and her knees draw up towards her torso under the blankets but they can only go so far and the bed rattles with the effort.

I try to get a hold of myself but I can't catch my breath, I'm too frightened to move. I should get out of the room.

Maeve, I think. I need Maeve.

Mam looks down to her wrists and I look, too, and see how the skin has come away. She's pulling away from the bed so recklessly that the twine is biting into her grey skin, through the muscles and it keeps going. A thick wine-coloured mess is leaking from her – from *its* – wrists but Mam keeps coming and something gives way. I don't know whether it is the string that breaks or my mother's own flesh and bone, but she – no it, it – *it* has an arm free and it reaches—

I find my voice and I scream.

I know Maeve'll be close.

And only now, at last, do I remember my knives and I pull one free from its sheath and I drop it but my clawing fingers pick it up off the ground and I tell my shaking pathetic legs to stand, to *stand*, to – fuck and I'm up, quivering but moving. I get to the door, inch by stupid inch, which has been open anyway this whole time and I know I can leave this room and vault the stairs and be out of the house in the time it'll take her to get the rest of the way free and to come for me.

Still, I stand there, the tip of the knife cool between my fingers, my body falling at last into a guard position, and I wait for Maeve to come and tell me what to do.

One of her legs is free now and she's half off the bed. The metal frame moves with her as she bites the air and reaches for me with clawed hands. I back up slowly, one leg moving quietly behind the other, light on my feet now, but my eyes never leaving it, the enemy.

'Maeve!' I shout again.

If I let loose this knife would she go down? Can I do this violence?

I hear Maeve at last, at the bottom of the stairs, coming up. I won't take my eyes off the skrake even to glance at her, but she puts her hand on my shoulder and I feel her looking me up and down to see how close I let Mam get, to see am I bitten.

'All right?' she says. Her voice is not flat. It's not emotionless, but it's calm. It makes me feel angry.

'No!' I say, the tears starting again. 'Maeve, help her!'

'You don't need my help,' she says smoothly, answering a whole other question I haven't asked.

I lift my eyes up off the target and I look at her.

'Keep your eyes on the skrake,' she says, nodding towards my mother, still snarling towards us, making slow progress, the twine on the hand that's still tied to the bed cutting her badly.

'Loose your weapon,' Maeve advises, and I feel her look at me when I don't line up my aim. 'Go on,' she says, her voice hardening.

'No,' I tell her. 'I won't.' I fall out of my guard and let my throwing hand drop.

Maeve looks at me again, and I look back at her, trying to match her hardness, her steadiness. After a while she looks away and sighs.

She steps into the bedroom, towards the skrake.

'Maeve!' I shout, and bring my knife up again, ready to throw.

The skrake reaches for her with its one ruined arm, and Maeve deftly sidesteps and stabs the skrake in the neck with a blade I didn't even know she had in her fist. I scream loud and hard and good, a scream of shock and grief, but my mother doesn't die. She falters and gurgles and chokes. She keeps reaching for Maeve, who takes one step back towards the door and looks at me coldly.

'Now will you kill it?'

I am sobbing. I shake my head in squeamish revulsion, so hard I might be trying to loose water out of my ears. My stomach twists. Maeve moves forwards lightly and stabs again, quick and hard, in and out like breathing. Mam writhes and screeches.

'Now?'

I'm crying too hard to speak, so Maeve steps forwards again and plunges her knife into the heart of the skrake straight through the soft material of the cleanish shirt I'd put on her only yesterday. My mother roars and twists. She sounds just like herself. The knife wedges for a moment but Maeve pulls hard and is free and as she pulls out her knife the blood pours out of the wound and my mother seems to moan.

'Finish this,' Maeve says.

I take a half-step forwards without meaning to but I'm still shaking my head – I can't, I can *not*.

Maeve steps forwards again towards her and stabs again, and then again.

With each new injury my mother looks more frightened. She screams.

I take another step forwards, and another, while Maeve brutalises my mother and shouts at me to kill her.

I cannot kill her; I must make this end.

I bring my knife to the string that tethers my mother's wrist to the bed.

'Maeve,' I say, and I see her eyes widen as she watches me cut through. My mother lunges forwards, three feet closer to Maeve in a heartbeat, and it is all she can do to jump back; she gets her hand to my mother's head, avoiding her fingernails narrowly, and she smashes her stabbing knife into Mam's skull.

The skrake, my mother, sighs as she dies and I listen for my name but do not hear it. I am kneeling beside her ruined, ragged body, half in and half out of the bed, too frightened to touch her or let her rest again on her bloody mattress, but unable to leave her. Trapped, as usual.

After a little while I begin to hear the silence in the room, and then Maeve's jagged breathing in it. Our eyes meet for a moment and I'm nearly surprised by the sadness in hers before they fall away from my face and on to the floor.

Maeve gives a nod, one small movement of the head, and I know that she's taking in now what she's done, what I made her do because I could not.

I think somewhere beneath the tang of shit and the coppery scent of blood I can smell Mam's scent, lavender, mint and earth.

Chapter Twenty-Nine

I WAKE IN THE NIGHT SHIVERING AND SLICK FROM DREAMS of teeth and slug-like tongues. I hear Maeve calling for me and I'm awake, my hands reaching for my knives.

Cillian sleeps on, breathing evenly, his face a peaceful blank. We were too tired to eat or do anything but swallow some water and scoop away damp leaves to find dry earth to rest in. Every night it's easier to sleep beside him, to curl into the warmth of his body. That closeness helps the way we are during the day. I fold myself back into his warmth and shut my eyes again.

Later I wake again and look around in the half-light, surprised at where we are. From my memory, from my recollection of the country around us, with its markers of hills and small round ruined castles, we're further west than I'd have guessed. Home is not so far off now and the thought pinches my stomach. If we don't find the others in the next few days, will we turn back when we reach the sea and walk the road east again? Or will we keep going, Cillian and me, out past the waterfall in the little skiff to the island? I try to picture it: showing him the island and the house, eking out a life there, the two of us. Mam and Maeve would have been satisfied with it.

I leave him to sleep and go to the road to find space to stretch and exercise. I am stiff with the cold and it takes a long time to warm my muscles, to feel as if I'm fluid and strong and supple. After a while, Cillian joins me, and he sits at the side of the road going through his pack and watching mc as the sun comes up. He is keen to be off, I know, and he looks around him often. He should be watching for skrake but he's looking for his family.

'Are you going to teach me some of that?' Cillian passes me the canten.

'You want to learn?' I take a large swig. I feel OK. Good, nearly. My back pinches and screams a little less every day. The palms of my hands are more sore than skin but they'll heal, too.

'You don't have to live by the sword to die by the sword.'

I squint against the early sun. 'What is that?'

'I heard it somewhere. You don't have to know how to fight skrake to get killed by one, it means.'

I nod, considering, watching him while he packs up his gear again. It's nearly like something Maeve would say.

Cillian's nose is still swollen and he's skinny and tired-looking. He takes the canten off me and swallows deep draughts of water, with his head thrown back and his eyes closed. His neck is brown and dirty and soft but strong-looking and I have an urge to put my lips to the soft skin.

Instead, I get up and get moving. Cillian follows me. We have a good system now. We go quickly and quietly. Fairly quietly. Cillian's feet are noisy and he cannot manage his breath well. I wish he'd copy me, like I tried to copy Maeve and Mam while I was learning, but he's not paying enough attention and in fairness his nose is broke.

'Do you think they would have tried to leave markers?' I ask.

'Markers?'

It's hard for me to be patient.

'Signs? Made from sticks, maybe, or messages written with stones or in the dust.'

'Written? With words?'

I nod.

'They can't do that,' Cillian says then, in the same careful tone, and looking at me with his head tilted and his eyes narrowed.

'Nobody taught you to read or write?'

'Not that many in Phoenix City know letters – not women, anyway.'

'Why not the women?'

'Women have enough to be doing,' he says, as if I am not one. The easy way he says it, as if the words haven't passed through him but have only been skimmed over his surface.

Cillian is staring off towards the west. 'They were going to stop and wait and we'd catch them,' he is muttering. 'That was the plan.'

Cillian goes over it aloud to himself as we walk the road, more and more often, with disbelief in his voice. 'They're ahead of us or they're behind us: those are the only two options.'

Those are not the only two options, I think. There are way more. They could be anywhere at all. They could have seen something that tempted them off away from the road – water or shelter when they needed it. They could have been chased off, by skrake. They could have been worried about us, and turned back: we could be moving in opposite directions. They could be injured. They could be dead. They could be bitten and lying in ditches, shitting themselves and turning slowly.

The longer we go on, the longer we don't see them, the more likely these other options become, until eventually one of them will become a definite. I try to reach out with my senses, to intuit whether they're still on the road. I can't feel anything. My gut can tell me nothing, only it's tight with hunger again. Cillian is talking.

'Nic would be worried that we haven't caught up with her. Probably she moved fast at first. She always walks fast when she's angry. Then she'd slow down. If she moved off the road at all it wouldn't be for long, and she'd stay somewhere she could keep an eye on things.'

The way he's talking, I know he isn't really telling it to me. He's just saying the words out loud. And he's right, so he is. We could go back or we could keep going forwards.

'If we don't find them . . .' Cillian starts again. He is angry with me for being calm when he cannot be calm. I know because of the way it was with Maeve and me. Cillian's words sound like they're being squeezed out of him. 'If—' he tries again, and then a third time: 'If we don't . . .'

'We'll find them,' I tell him, without really meaning to. 'I'll help you.' I try to sound soft.

His eyes are looking for mine and I let him meet them. We look at each other for a long moment before I tear mine away.

'You'll stay with me?'

'Yes. You're the only person I know.'

He laughs a little, a messy, surprised laugh through his nose.

'If we leave signs for them like this, will they follow

them?' I ask, going to the side of the road for a stick draw an arrow in the dust.

He looks at it and thinks but only moves his shoulders up and down.

I try to imagine again what our lives would be like, intertwined, surviving together. His male presence on the island. I'd nearly forgotten these last few days I should be afraid of him. I think about his face and hands moving around in the house, in the bedroom next to mine. The shape of him in the garden, his hands on the fruit.

And then I think about the way he held on to Nic, the way he kissed her, and her swollen stomach, the way he was with Aodh. He'd never believe, our whole life, that leaving them out here on the road was the right thing to do, even if they're gone. My chest hurts and I'm not sure I can distinguish the different pains any more.

Our hands, between us as we sit side by side in the dirt, are so close. I could reach out and take his.

'We can't keep going on like this,' Cillian says at last. 'What will we do?'

'Quiet your voice,' I say. 'We should rest a while, and then we'll go on again,' I tell him. 'We'll leave arrows and go slower, we'll look more carefully for tracks.' I try to talk like Maeve, like I know exactly what I'm doing, but the way Cillian looks at me makes me wonder do either of us believe it.

We walk west all morning, slowly and looking about us carefully. The road starts curling around the last hill, the last until the land flattens out and the road ends and disperses into littler ones, leading back to the beach, back home, and we climb it for the view at the top.

The country spreads empty and wide around us. To the west we can make out a haze that hides the sea beyond.

'I'll see can I find more water,' I tell him. He's not listening to me, and we don't really need water, but I want to stretch out on my own a little. I want space to think. Cillian has his hands in his hair and he doesn't sit down, despite his exhaustion. Leaving him alone a little while may be no harm.

I work my way round the slope, breathing slowly and deeply. I listen hard for skrake, sometimes realising that what I'm hoping I'll hear is Danger's padded trot. I keep waiting to feel him nudge his nose into the palm of my hand. I grieve for him. It is easier to feel that sadness than to think about Maeve, or my mother, even.

I sit a long time, longer than I meant, and watch the country around me. Here there are no tall trees, only wind-swept shrub, low rock walls still exposed out of the dry brown earth. We're closer than I'd thought.

The last time I was close to something I wanted it didn't go well for me so it didn't.

From here I can just make out the broad grey strip of the

sea. I wonder has Cillian seen it too. The day is bright and dry. I know I'm staying away too long, that Cillian will be anxious. *Climbing the walls*, Mam would have said. I try again to feel out for Nic and Aodh, for where they might be, for what happened them. They're close by, or else they're dead. Would we go looking for their bodies, back along the road, the way I'd to go looking for Maeve? I lie back against the ground and close my eyes.

I smell it before I see it. Smoke. A plume, close by, thin but getting larger, billowing in the breeze. I scramble to my feet and run towards it, back to Cillian.

I find him where I left him, covered in dirt and soot, standing by the fire. He has gathered branches and leaves, everything he could find, and dragged it all to make a huge pyre.

'Put it out!' I shout over the crackling.

'I can't.' He wipes his hands on his thighs and looks full at me, his streaked face full of fear and excitement. 'I threw away our water.'

Chapter Thirty

I LIKE THE WAY THE WORLD FEELS JUST AS THE SUN IS COMING up. There's a quality to the pre-dawn quiet that is so different to the sullen roar behind the wind. It's *expectant*. The day smells fresh.

I only realise when we get going how petrified I've been my whole life, how I've been scared every moment of being alone and of being left on the island. I was tight like a fist, but when we get moving my fingers began to unfurl, to relax and then reach out.

Maeve made me pack for us and now my decisions have been made, and I could not have made better ones, no matter how bad they are. I'll know soon whether I'm strong enough for whatever there is, for this life.

I try to sleep the night before, knowing I'll need it, but only manage a doze when the darkness begins to soften. When it's light, I dress with my fresh-cleaned knives, a hat against the sun, layers against the cold.

Outside I give a low whistle and after a few moments the dog noses his way through the long grass around the house, tail wagging lazily.

Maeve came home one day, two summers after Mam died, with this big-pawed black dog and I felt a softness, a bit of *give* in the tightness in me, for the first time since.

I still hated her, but it was like hating a rock: she didn't care. She trained me hard but wouldn't speak a word otherwise, so she couldn't notice me ignoring her. Maeve was always quiet but after Mam she was silent in new ways. I went a bit mad, I think, and so did Maeve. Even still, apart from that, she knew I needed someone to talk to, and somehow she found something that'd suit.

'He'll be useful,' she'd said and I'd looked at her properly in the light for the first time in a long time. She was getting old. The light in her eyes had gone and her skin was papery and pale. She got old all at once after Mam died. 'He can warn us if people are coming.'

She was so unused to speaking she'd trouble making the words; they were slurred in her mouth. Anyway it seemed cruel then to point out that nobody was ever coming, so I stayed quiet.

It's a problem all on its own, so it is; we're to be afraid of people, and we need them.

All Maeve needed really was Mam. Even Mam and Maeve together weren't going to be enough for me, not for ever.

I wonder about where she found Danger to bring him home to me. Not on this island. She'd a habit, after Mam, of leaving, of going off in the skiff on her own without bothering to tell me and I wouldn't see her for days. I nearly missed her when she was gone, even with the distance between us, and then she'd be back and I'd to face her silence and her misery in person, and I'd realise I still missed her. Maeve was off looking for Mam even when she was sitting in the same room as me.

I can nearly feel now when she's thinking about taking off. I'll catch her sometimes, and follow her down to the skiff, watch as she casts off and wonder will I see her again. She's nobody with her to bring her back if she's caught, and every time she goes it seems more likely she'll meet her own end out there.

In the meantime I only get stronger and more desperate to get the fuck off the island.

It was only after she brought the dog back with her that I started feeling like I could speak again, and I used my speak to tell her, not for the first time but for the first time in years, that I wanted to go with her. It had been the plan anyway, it always was. I was full-grown and it was past time. Even still, she shook her head and I cried and we went back to not speaking. The feelings settled and fixed. Days passed slow and unchanging while the years bunched together and wasted, so fast.

Danger and I head down to the beach together. The dog trots ahead of me, pausing every now and then to make sure I'm coming, and when his eyes catch mine his wagging tail goes a bit faster. Watching him makes me feel lighter.

I breathe in the air, warm now, but the coolest it'll be for the next twelve hours, and break into a little jog along the sand. Soon Danger is panting. Maeve – the old Maeve – is in my ear saying I can't slow down, I have to keep pushing. *The minute you slow down, that's the same minute they'll get you.*

I leave myself a few moments to look at the waves. I won't see them tomorrow, and that knowledge is strange after a lifetime of routine. I love this beach. It hadn't occurred to me, really, that I'd miss it, and now I can't stop thinking about what makes Slanbeg home. I try not to pause over Mam, or even about the way Maeve used to be, as a rule, but now I can't keep my thoughts away from them. I was a stupid child and a pain, probably, but oh I was loved.

I get angry sitting there thinking away to myself. I'm so aggrieved at what I had and lost, of all the things ruined before we even got here. People had enough to eat and drink, and work to do, and families, and hot water coming out of the tap and toilets that'd cart all your shit off away so you didn't even have to think about where next to dig a latrine. And you could get in an aeroplane or a boat and go anywhere in the whole wide world you liked and there'd be whole other groups of people, whole communities there. I can nearly understand the hunger of the skrake, thinking about that. The desperation of having *nothing* and needing needing needing.

All we're left with is this broken place, and emptiness that starts in the fractured sky and torn earth but ends with this hollowness in my chest, and a fear of what the hell is out there. All the things Maeve told me about, and especially those things that she hasn't. There's acres within me I know nothing about and I won't ever learn unless I get away from Slanbeg.

It makes me *furious*, thinking about it all.

The anger is helpful, though, I'm after finding. Anger's more useful than sadness or fear. I hold it tight to me: I shape it into plans. I keep my teeth biting into each other and my fists curled tight. I want to pound them on something again and again until that thing is nothing more than the sand on this beach.

Chapter Thirty-One

I KICK DIRT ON TO THE FIRE, BUT CILLIAN GETS IN MY WAY and keeps getting in the way.

I think about putting him down and maybe I should've, and it'd have been easy to crunch my knuckles again into his pretty cheek, but I don't. When it's clear I won't be able to put out the blaze I take him by the wrist and drag him away down the hill.

After a little while he runs with me back to the road and over it and on a little, but then he stops again and won't go any further. With threats and sense I get him behind a bush at least, and we stay there, in the dirt, waiting and watching the fire. Our funeral pyre.

This is how we die, I keep thinking.

At least I saw something in my life.

At least I'm not alone.

I hope with all my great might that we'll find them: two lonely figures dragging their feet on the road ahead of us, or crying out to us from behind. Half the country must be able to see the smoke coming off this hill. We only see the empty road, though, green hills around us and half-swallowed buildings.

'They'll see it,' Cillian keeps saying. 'I know they'll see it.'

Maybe it'll even work. I imagine if it was me and Maeve. We'd have just looked at each other before she put her sparker to some kindling and that look would have meant 'Good luck', and 'This is the right thing to do, we have agreed', and 'Remember your JICs' and even 'I love you'.

Crouched down in the bush, I talk to Cillian. I talk to him about where to go if we get separated. I tell him as well as I can how to find Slanbeg, just in case, and I make him repeat it to me, again and again. I give him the thing he's wanted off me since he first saw me.

And, just in case, I give him a knife, and I show him how to hold it. I think for a moment about showing him something defensive, something simple like a front kick, but he's shaking and wide-eyed already. He'll do well to hang on to the information he has.

I try to smile because there's nothing else for it now. I won't leave him.

'It'll be OK,' I say. I bite back at the anger I feel coursing around my innards; I tell it to wait.

We're covered well enough in the undergrowth. We've a clear path behind us: we can run if hiding doesn't suit us. We can separate, and we'll double back and meet here, or three klicks down the road, at the shady place we can see in the distance, or beyond that, on the beach. We have shared out the things in Cillian's pack. If we can't find each other, we'll continue west, and we can leave each other messages in the dust. He'd find his way to Slanbeg if he has to without me, maybe, to my little skiff hidden behind some rocks on a stony beach beside cliffs that are bright pink in the morning. So close to home now, and so far.

I shouldn't have left him alone. There wasn't a rule for that in training unless it was *beware people*. How he managed to get together so much kindling is a credit to him. I wonder how he lit it – some little tool hidden away in his pack, maybe.

We stay quiet. I worry. We should call it off, move further down the road, get away from all the evils coming our way. But Cillian wouldn't come and there's no point to saying any of it.

So, we stay.

* * *

215

We're a good while into our vigil before there is movement: a skrake, a long way off but rising the hill towards the fire. From this distance it's hard to see, but I can tell from the way it moves. Cillian goes rummaging again in his pack and I'm nearly ready to whisper to him to shut up but instead watch as he looks through one end of the machine he takes out. He sighs a long, shaking breath, and then hands it to me. I put the thing to my eye the way he did and for a moment see nothing but a blur of green, brown and blue but then I see it, the skrake, as if it's up close.

The person it was has gone totally, disappeared beneath a layer of mostly decayed skin, so that I can guess almost nothing about the host, not even the gender. A type of spiderweb-like fungus or growth has spread around the worst affected parts of the body: the head, especially the mouth and eyes, and underarms, the groin. What is left of the clothing is dark. The hair clings in clumps to the scalp, but the skrake's head is just a mess of rot and teeth. The mouth hangs open, the jaw nearly gone, and from it protrudes the wet-looking, slug-like growth, the teeth around it. I swallow.

The skrake moves quickly with odd, half-jerking, half-fluid motions. I watch the way it moves its feet: I want to be able to track one, if I lose the run of myself and go chasing after one some day. If I survive this, which is feeling unlikely. The skrake makes its twitching way up the hill and approaches the fire, too quickly, limbs flailing out rapidly. It seems to almost walk into the flames before jerking away again.

In our hiding place, something touches my hand and I flinch away reflexively. Cillian doesn't take his eyes off the skrake but he puts his damp hand into mine and I look at his pale, frightened face, I drink it in, before tearing my eyes back towards the fire.

The skrake is still but for one jerking arm, its head pointed towards us. It couldn't have heard that small movement from this far away. I hold my breath. It *couldn't*. The slug-like thing coming out of the host's mouth seems to strain towards us. But then there is a noise to our left, from the west. After a moment I can make out movement through the trees. I hear it then, a throat-deep scratching noise, nearly voiceless, carried on the wind.

The *sound* of it.

They shuffle along, one after the other, within a few hundred metres of us. Cillian squeezes my hand so tight it hurts but we don't shift otherwise: I try not even to blink. I could take one full-grown skrake, maybe, with a little luck or a little help. I count four, including the one already at the fire. A small thread of wind drifts by us and we can smell them on it. Rank and rotten-sweet, the kind of stench that'd keep the appetite off you for a week.

Time passes. The clouds are beginning to roll in and

soon it will begin to rain and the fire will go out. I wonder if maybe no more will come and these four won't see us and we'll be able to get away after all. The smoke is what really counts, though, and it spirals high into the sky. If Aodh and Nic are alive and anywhere near us, they will see it. Cillian was right about that much.

There are five skrake now at the fire and we keep watching as they pitch and flail around it. They twitch, run a few steps in one direction and then back again. Their heads turn with sudden movements and are tilted on one side, like they're listening for something. They limp and stumble but do not fall. Their stomachs are bloated, their legs and arms are thin, worn down almost to the bone. Their mouths open and close and I watch as the protrusions work back and forwards from between their teeth, sometimes coming forwards, glistening under the sun, as if searching for something or tasting the air, then retreating again. I see mouths open and close, jaws chomping.

They're desperate, demented, starving. Teeth gnash together, snapping at thin air, and the protrusions come out again. You can nearly see the way it'd happen, the growth in the throat after a bite, filling up the whole body till it's just a skin. The monster inside, all hunger and violence with nothing else left. Just the way Mam and Maeve said it to me.

I drag my eyes away from the monsters and watch

instead for two human figures, frightened and looking for us. We'll have to see them first, if they are coming, to stop them. I'm not sure Cillian has thought of this.

Time passes. Maybe these five skrake are the only ones that happen to be within sight or smell of our fire. Perhaps seeing them is all we will achieve, and now we'll have to take to the road again, to—

I haven't finished my thought before I see more coming down the road from the east. There is one, then two behind that, and behind that four, all together, all moving quickly. After a few heartbeats, I hear more screeches, to the north, ahead of us. We're nearly surrounded.

'Move,' I breathe to Cillian. He lets go my hand and I work my knuckles stiffly. We move quietly backwards; we do not panic. We progress slowly and quietly, on our bellies first and then on hands and knees. We are silent; our noise cannot compete with the fire's. We creep south-west cautiously, stopping every dozen steps or so to listen hard. The skrake are moving all around us. We stay low, and here off the road we're mostly under good cover.

There are so many of them.

I'm biting back the fright and I can feel Cillian shaking beside me.

We keep moving.

We have circled half-way back to the road when a skrake making for the fire sees us. I've a knife flying through the air and buried nicely in its throat before I can think. The skrake slows but doesn't stop. I watch for the time it takes to breathe in once and already there is another behind it, going quick.

We move.

We try to keep quiet but that means slow going and the skrake is gaining on us. If we stop to fight it, to kill it, we'll make noise and more will come. From a dozen choices, we've only one now. One bad option.

'Go!' I tell Cillian, and we both stand up straight and get our legs going.

We run flat out, noisily, smashing through whatever we need to. Skrake heading towards the fire, coming from the north and the south, hear us and see us. By the time we make it back on to the road I'd guess we have six or seven behind us: I will not snap my head back to check, I will not pause.

Ten minutes ago we felt nearly safe. Now we're running for our lives. *Things change fast*, I think as I run, and it's half Maeve's voice and half my own in my head.

Now that we are on the road the going is easier: we move quicker, but so do the skrake, and if there are more in front of us, we'll get trapped between them. There are buildings to either side of us, a small village almost. Ahead of us, another klick or so down the road, there's a sharp turn to the left and I hope that if we can get ahead of them enough we can lose them around it. Maybe they'll get distracted by the flames of the fire; maybe they'll be drawn back to the heat. We could throw ourselves into the undergrowth, lie still: if they cannot see us or hear us or smell us, maybe they won't know that we're there. That was our Just-In-Case for if we were being chased down the road by a load of skrake. It's laughable now, ridiculous.

We round the corner and beside me I hear Cillian cry out, a gurgling, ugly sound in the midst of his exhausted breath. Even as I glance at him I hear another cry, answering his, from further down the narrowing road to the east.

Ahead of us on the road, holding hands, are Nic and Aodh.

Chapter Thirty-Two

I'D TAKE OUT THE LITTLE SKIFF WHENEVER I FELT THAT Maeve wouldn't be looking for it and rowed east, a bit further every time, scaring myself shitless. The last summer I'd got so far that I could make out a hulking dark shape in the mist ahead; landmass. Ireland. I'd turned round and rowed straight home again, elated and terrified. Then the weather had turned and winter came on and there were months and months of stewing in the house and on the island. When summer came around again though nothing would have frightened me off.

I never knew how but she was waiting for me at the little jetty. She had hidden the boat and I might have ditched the bag and swum for it only she said we'd go together.

'Where are you going, warrior.' Maeve doesn't need to ask questions; the question is a monotone demand and more words than she has said to me in a long time.

'I can't stay here, I can't stay for ever,' is all I can answer her. I try to soften it: 'I was only going to go for a few hours, for a day. I'd come back.' It is the truth.

She looks down at her feet and it's the closest she's ever come to backing down.

'It isn't enough,' I tell her, making a helpless gesture at the woods, the sea.

Maeve gives an almost imperceptible nod. I watch her struggle and relent, or resign, or give up, maybe. In it I hear her thinking that she should never have let me know about the skiff; she should have told me the sea was full of sharks.

'You're so like your mam,' she says.

It takes me a small while to get the hang of rowing properly, but Maeve shows me a few strokes and then I'm steady enough and enjoying the breeze against the sweat on my skin. I watch the woods, the whole island, begin to get smaller. With every pull I'm a little further away from everything I've known in my life. I'm a little freer.

I pause to balance my hat further back on my head, guarding the back of my neck against the sun, and breathe, and smile. I am the very happiest I have been since Mam died. I can feel the closeness of the winter, the frustration of the months and years of toil and worry lift off me in layers till I feel light and free. I tug on the oars harder, loving the feel of the wood in my hands and the breeze in our hair and the sense there's a whole world beneath us in the sea and another ahead of us, a world we're to join at last.

I'm sweating hard by the time the sun is a hand-width up from the horizon. I row another half-hand-width before the ruined bridge that used to attach the island to the mainland appears above us. It is menacing; the hulking broken shadow of it is spooky and sad. People died up there. Right up there above me, leathered skin dries and shies back away from bones.

I rub Danger's head softly in this breathing moment, it is so good to be alive. Better down here, still trying, than up there. I crack my knuckles and set to again and we move off towards the mist crowding the coast.

I row for a long time. Strong as I am, I know my arms will be sore come tomorrow.

Tomorrow.

Never has the word held such excitement for me, such terror. Who knows where we'll be, tomorrow.

Chapter Thirty-Three

I SHOUT AT THEM SO THAT CILLIAN DOES NOT HAVE TO.

'RUN!'

Quick as we're going, frightened as I am, I can make out the full spectrum of Nic's expressions. Delight, then fear, then, admirably fast, grim determination. She tosses her stick to the side of the road and starts to back away, bringing Aodh with her by the hand. They don't start running, though, till we're nearly on top of them. Nic reaches out to Cillian, to touch him, as if she needs to make sure that he's real. I meet her eyes just for a moment: her face looks drawn and dirty and happy and *petrified*.

I am glad, so glad, to see them.

The four of us we run west together.

We move through a small village. It might offer some cover if only we had more space between us and the skrake. I risk a glance behind. I count eight. I throw my eyes over my left shoulder and count again. Nine and maybe more coming. Way too many.

My legs still feel strong as we run away and out from the little village, due west. I focus on my breathing. I'm going all right, I feel fit. I'm a little ahead of Cillian and Aodh now and I check my speed. Aodh is quick but she's small, she won't be able to keep up this pace for long. Nic is pregnant but she is strong. Running for two. I'm the only one of us with training.

I focus on my breathing, make it smooth and regular, get myself steady. I know how long I can keep this speed up – a long time – and this knowledge is important, it gives confidence. The others, they don't know how far they can run and that scares them. They're tired already and that is frightening, too. They're not used to being uncomfortable like this.

Rage burns, sudden and bright. They're weaker than me and they'll slow me down because nobody trained them and because they didn't bother train themselves. What sort of world do they think we live in? The anger feels good. I could run all day.

I check my speed again, make sure I'm bringing up the rear, and try to keep an eye on the road ahead as well. If there are more ahead of us coming this way, we'll have to peel off the road. We run on. Behind us I can still see a snake of black smoke rising high into the sky. It'll rain soon.

Aodh slows almost to a stop. Her face is coiled up in pain. She moves forwards slowly, stumbling and holding her side, half doubled-over. I snatch looks at the road; it won't be long now.

Cillian throws his bag to the ground and hunkers down in front of Aodh. She climbs on to his back and Cillian moves off, slow and working hard but keeping going. It's nearly seamless and I feel humbled by his thinking.

The thought of leaving her had already occurred to my traitor brain, the part of it that works through situations and comes out with an answer of what it'll take to survive. The trained part. And in the meantime here's Cillian picking her up, carrying her.

Nic is stooping to pick up Cillian's pack but I put out my hand and snatch it from her. She's enough to carry. I get a look at her face as I pull the bag from her and our eyes meet for a horrible moment. She is pure fear, near panic.

I start running again but she isn't behind me.

'Come on!' I shout to Nic. She is stock-still on the road, looking back towards what is chasing us. Frozen by it. I go back, cursing, and take her by the wrist and I pull hard until she is stumbling beside me again, slower even than Cillian.

It takes a while before Aodh can run again. I can feel how she hates being carried, child though she is. She lets go her hold as soon as she's able and is off Cillian's back and we speed up again, Nic pushing herself hard. As we run Cillian reaches to take his bag back off me and I hesitate but give it him. No one spares their breath for talk. What would we say? Run faster.

The road has risen on a small hill that gives a view of the land behind us. I turn and slow my pace, take two deep, shuddering breaths. Cillian is still moving but looking back at me.

'Come on!' he shouts.

'I'll catch up, keep moving!'

They keep moving.

It takes my eyes a moment to focus. There, there is the village we passed through, in the distance, a few shadowy right angles. And there is the road leading from that point to this. I follow it with my eyes. It disappears round a bend, reappears, curves to the left. I see nothing. Can we have lost them? My eye catches on something. There is movement. Figures, moving fast, a few front-runners and then more, bunched together. More than nine now. They are still coming. They are moving faster than we are.

We don't have much time.

I turn and run again, pumping my legs faster to catch up with Cillian and Aodh, and to feel how much strength they've left in them. I don't know if I can really hear them – feet on the road, limping, dragging, pattering – or I'm just imagining it.

I take another look over my shoulder.

They are just a few hundred metres away.

It's amazing we got this far, the four of us.

So close to the beach, and not nearly close enough.

Cillian stops suddenly, puts down his bag. He takes his knife, the big knife I lent him, and positions himself in the middle of the road. His ragged breaths shake his whole body.

'Cillian!' I shout. Aodh and I are on the road ahead of him, slowed but not stopped. Aodh is already crying beside me. She knows. Cillian turns to look. The smile he contrives for her is like a miracle.

'Be good,' he says.

Nic is screaming. She throws herself at him, grabs whatever she can grab, his arms, his clothes, and tugs hard. She's incoherent, bawling. I feel my eyes prickle and I move forwards, take her by the wrist again and I move her away. Crying, she breaks free and throws her arms around Cillian's neck and for a moment he is swayed. He closes his eyes, and puts his arms around her and for a moment they stay like that, silent. Then Cillian thrusts Nic from him and turns back to face the road. I grab her and together we start moving away, Nic sobbing, me pulling.

Cillian looks at me, gives me one sure, firm nod. He is trusting me with their lives – all three of them. He is entrusting me with his own, too, in a way; that I'll make sure he's not giving it up for nothing. He turns away from me, from us, towards the skrake.

I am so frightened.

Aodh, Nic and I run on. Nic is running by herself now, but so slowly, with one arm over her belly. I push everything out of my brain but breathing and moving and keeping Aodh beside me. I'm sure I can smell the sea when I next hear the sound of many footsteps running behind us. I cry out, try to pick up the speed, reach for Aodh's hand and drag her with me. I don't want to look behind us now. My breath is coming in ragged gasps and Aodh is nearly done for.

I see the sign I've been looking for at last, a mark I made days ago – a lifetime ago – a rough 'M', for Mam, for Maeve, scraped into the metal. I lead us off the road and on to a smaller one and we keep going.

We have run for such a long time.

I let myself hope a little that we'd lose them, that they might keep going straight instead of following us, but after a little while on the smaller road, working our way round trees and bushes, I hear them move behind us. Next it will be my turn to lay down my own life. I'm thankful that I have the ability to do that, the will, but even now there is some selfishness at work, too. I'm glad I won't be the last one left alive.

We run till Nic falls to her hands and knees in the middle of the road, panting hard. Tears have made tracks in her filthy face. Snot bubbles around her nose and her eyes are red and raw.

'Keep moving,' she says, her voice a rasp. 'I can't.'

I shake my head; she has two lives and I have just one.

'You can save Aodh,' she says. 'I can't.'

'Not yet,' I say, 'not yet. Get up – we're nearly home.'

Chapter Thirty-Four

MAEVE GOT BIT THAT TIME, THAT FIRST TIME WE WENT out to the mainland.

Nearly exactly three years after Mam died, so it was. I'm not sure she'd have wanted to linger longer, even for me.

We've been walking for a few hours inland, Maeve and me and the dog, when Maeve says to stop and show her where we are exactly. I open up the map and she hunkers down on the ground and shields her eyes from the glare of the sun. I've one thick, dirty finger on the old paper, tracing the blue of the road. The big blue lines are still OK to trust, Maeve says. She's different now, off-island, more awake, brighter in herself.

I stop and look around us again. Mostly the land is like

on Slanbeg: green and brown and flat, cowering underneath the sky above it.

'Show me where we are,' Maeve tells me, and I crouch beside her in the dust.

It's an old map, Maeve has explained to me before, and I know that things won't match up exactly: the smaller roads anyway have mostly been swallowed up by the woods, and maybe even the courses of rivers have changed, but I know where home is. I know the straight high road that goes all the way east.

I try to guess how far we'd have come along the road. Beside me, Maeve has stood to stare about us real obvious to let me know that this is serious and that I should be doing the same thing when I'm not looking at the map. She crouches again to look at the point I'd put my finger on, a spot nearly in the middle of Ireland and I take my turn to throw my eyes around at the barren landscape. Doing it even more obviously. To poke fun, but to show her I'm on it as well, I'm ready.

'No,' Maeve says, 'look again.'

It turns out that we've walked about a quarter of what I thought. At this rate it would take four or five days to get to the east coast, and that's if the map is mostly right. Not that Maeve would ever let us head east, I'd guess. That's where Phoenix City is, off in that direction, somewhere towards or near Dublin. Only Maeve knows now.

'Think now about where to aim for tonight, where we'll make camp.'

I don't want her to think things are fixed just because she's talking, just because we're here now, though if I was asked why I was so angry with her still I don't know could I say.

I want to go east just so we can walk that road a little, and nearly point at a town some distance down the blue line in front of us, but in the end I put my hands behind my back and stare her out.

Maeve maybe doesn't notice or maybe doesn't care. She shakes her head beside me. 'Too many places to hide in a town, too hard to keep an eye out for ourselves. Beware tall buildings,' and I stiffen up in annoyance because I've heard her say it a million times, but on she goes. 'They're liable to falling down. We're headed south.' She's murmuring to herself, her words, now they're coming, tumbling out of her. Her voice is scratchy. 'We'll have to get through the town to stay on this road, and this road is the right one for meeting up with the bigger road. That'll take us . . . here. We don't want to be going through the village just when it's getting dark.'

She gives a little nod at last. 'Let's camp here,' and she points to a stretch of blue beside a bend in the river. I can see how it's a good place. If we're lucky we'll be able to get off the road and get fresh water.

Danger gives a great yawn and thwaps his tail on the ground.

'Move out.'

I concentrate on keeping up, keeping my eyes on the road and trying not to get distracted by the changing landscape around us.

Maeve walks with purpose. She leans heavily on her stick but her strides are strong. She is light on her feet, tense and quiet. There's power in her yet.

I try to be quiet and vigilant. I try to be like Maeve even while I'm raging at her.

We stop to eat when the sun's at its highest and hottest, taking shelter in the long shadows of a rough patch of ramshackle houses. I use a bit of plastic to water the dog and we watch as he laps. It's so good to sit, to flex my arms and to look at things that I have never seen before.

We each eat a potato and I eat two eggs and I am about as close to full as I get. I watch carefully to make sure Maeve eats her share. She's had a cough and I can hear her wheeze. She hasn't shaken off the winter yet. We make ourselves comfortable and well hidden under some trees and I doze in the warmth, Danger curled up beside my legs.

After lunch the sun is on our backs and for a while the going feels easier. Once, late in the afternoon, I don't pay enough attention and trip over my own feet, going flying, skinning my knees. Maeve stops and turns to watch me pick myself up, and after that we stop more often for water and to eat a little, and to sit. I am young and strong, I can feel the strength in myself, waiting to be proven. And Maeve is old now, and a small bit sick, and still and all it is she who slows herself to wait for me.

That's what I remember most about all of that. The brief period I was happy, in between my mother dying and Maeve dying. A few hours on the mainland when I felt safe, when I felt like we had escaped something, and knew we were a family despite everything.

Chapter Thirty-Five

A FAST SHUFFLE IS ALL WE CAN MANAGE NOW. AODH IS limping and I pick her up and carry her, bent over my shoulder. It cannot be comfortable but she is still except for her breathing, in a half-faint. I know I cannot bring her far.

Nic is behind us, but still moving. I'll need to put Aodh down and get myself between her and the skrake, but I want to hold out as long as we can, until we're on the beach or a little closer at least. I can hear shouts, but I haven't the heart to turn. It's all I can do to put one step in front of another with Aodh weighing me down. Maeve's voice is in my ear, telling me to stop my whinging. *Why did you ever leave the island if you were going to give up here?* I keep going. I try to gauge how much energy I can keep in reserve for what must come next.

We keep moving, the three of us.

The two of us, and Nic not far behind.

At last, at long last, here is the beach. Aodh collapses on to the sand and I look for the skiff. For a few sickening moments I cannot see it but there it is, half hidden behind rocks and in the mist, where another person left it, ages ago.

I scream at Aodh to come and help me, and now she has her breath she's able to get up and get it moving with me down the shore. Between breaths, I tell her to get into the boat, to put her hands to the oars. To row south-west. Go fast, then go slow and easy, save your strength. Find the big cliffs on the edge of the sea, I tell her. Listen for the waterfall, you'll hear it, and row due west. Go under the broken bridge and you'll see the island at the other end.

Be safe there.

Find our ghost-town and ghost-house. Be alone for ever.

No.

Not alone.

I get Aodh into the boat and tell her to wait as long as she can. She cries and blinks at me uncomprehendingly, but I'm gone, tearing back off up the beach, my wet feet heavy and pinching.

I find Nic sitting in the middle of the road, looking on

calmly. Her hair flows over one shoulder, her eyes are languid now and without fear. She is surprised to see me. There is a skrake, a single one ahead of all the others, closing in.

'Come on,' I shout, pulling at her hands.

She shakes me off. 'There isn't time,' she says, her voice even, and the skrake has a third of the distance between us covered already.

'There is, there *is*!' I get my hands under her arms and tug till she's up, take her hand and half pull her along until she's running with me. She's not quick but she's not winded any more. I just need to get them away: we just need a little more time.

'Nic!' Aodh's thin voice carries across the beach, and Nic hears her and moves faster. We get to the shore, but that skrake, it's on us.

There isn't a moment to lose, not a second.

'Get in, get in,' Aodh shouts, and awkwardly Nic gets into the boat.

It's the look on her face as she sits and faces the shore that stops me: a stillness comes over it, with her eyes – they're blue, I notice for the first time – looking over my shoulder at something. Her hand, reaching to help me in, stops in mid-air, and her eyes come to meet mine, and I feel it then, the rotten meaty breath on the back of my neck.

Nic and Aodh scream and I begin to push, using the last of my strength now to get the skiff moving and into the water, but I can't, it's too heavy on the sand. I shout in frustration and shove, I give it everything and then it gives and it's moving.

Get ready, Maeve says in my ear.

I turn round to meet it and it flattens me into the sand and water.

I'd forgotten, nearly, how strong they were, how weighty. I can't breathe. The water is cold and merciless, up my nose and stinging my eyes.

Suddenly, with a *thwack*, it's off me and I'm up.

Standing unsteadily in the skiff, Nic has an oar in her hands, a smudge of brownish skrake blood stains the paddle.

The skrake is moving again, up before I can blink, and it's going now for the boat. I dive at it, grab it around the middle and hold on.

'GO!' I yell, my voice garbled and my mouth still half full of saltwater.

'No!' cries Aodh, still holding out her hands towards me and the skrake, but Nic, her eyes on mine, sits down hard. She begins grimly to pull.

It is all I can do to hold on to the skrake. Nic hit it so hard I can feel the blood welling down out of the side of its skull over my arms, into the cold clean water. I hold on for dear life.

I watch them go, the mist swallowing them up.

The skrake shakes and shudders and turns at last its attention to me.

I get ready.

I let it go suddenly, spring away towards the beach, and get down in a guard position. It comes for me and I leap, my knife in my hand already, and I go for the wound Nic made in its skull and I get my knife in there and the skrake goes down. Half in the water I keep it there, down, my knees on its arms, and I take my knife and I keep stabbing till it stops moving and then I look about me again.

It's only a miracle the rest of the horde haven't caught up with me yet: what new trick did Cillian pull out of that bag?

I get up off the skrake and back on to dry sand to get ready. I look behind me once more to the sea. To turn my face once more towards home, to Mam's bones in the ground there.

The little boat is making good progress, rowing hard as they can. Still in sight, but further than anyone could swim quickly. Nearly safe.

I tried, Mam, I did.

I can hear the rest of the horde. I make sure my knives are free and easily to hand. Just two left, then my dagger.

I finger the missing sheath and wonder did the knife I gave Cillian do him any good.

I blink away tears and try to think of something good,

something I can take with me. I think about my mother's humming, and running with Danger to the fingers on the beach at home. The way it feels when the curve of my leg lands just right in a kick. I think of Maeve, every day of my life, making me safe, and making me strong. For this, maybe. One life for two. For three, with luck.

I think about the soft look Cillian had while he slept.

My breath slows and I take one good lungful, in and out, and then another, and with my eyes still closed I bring a knife smooth and easy up as far as my ear.

In just about every way, I think dying will be easier than living.

'Come *on* ta fuck,' I say, though only moments have passed, really, and the first of them is nearly in range.

'COME ON,' I shout, and the feel of my voice in my throat makes me stronger. If I fight like I have never fought before, I could bring down a couple with me. I could aim for their legs, mangle them just, slow them down. I bring down my hands, flexing my fingers, trying to get more blood into them after our afternoon of running.

The skrake limp and sprint, climbing over one another, arms outstretched already for my flesh and in their overgrown fingernails I can feel the meat of me being torn from my bones with ripping tearing jagged teeth.

It's very real, now, my own death. I am terrified.

I see seven and probably there are more running behind

them. I close my eyes and the back of my eyelids shows me a noisy picture of skrake devouring Cillian: tearing into the soft tender flesh of his belly while he screams. I breathe deeply, in and out, trying to quell the shake in my fingers.

I am not frightened, I think. I'm *furious*.

I know where to put the anger, anyway, I feel it flexing along my muscles like fire.

I breathe once more. In. Out. I try to appreciate the feeling, to savour it.

It's raining. How long has it been raining?

Then the first is in range. Even as I lift my hand I think I could have raised it five seconds earlier; I have already made a mistake here. I aim at the nearest skrake, let fly, and hit the eye. It squirms and falters but doesn't stop.

There are way too many.

I remember I don't have to beat them, I just have to slow them down, make them forget to go looking for anyone else a while. Give them time. Pull hard, I think. I find the anger and the fire.

Fight hard, Maeve tells me.

They come faster now, and I reach again for a knife – I'll just have my dagger – but before I can get it away, oh so quickly and all at once they're on top of me, their fingers – their claws – reach for me, and one goes for me hard, lands on top of me.

The air is throttled out of me as I fall backwards on to the hard sand.

I think of my mother as I feel teeth bite down. My toes curl in pain and I can taste blood in my mouth and I scream and push the skrake hard, feeling my own skin and gristle rip and tear and burn.

I become aware of other noises but they're far away, unimportant. The only reality is the burning pain in my ear, the blood rushing in my head, the death waiting for me.

The weight of the horde, the mass lifts; after a moment there is just one. Someone is shouting – two people, more.

There are people, I think, but my thinking is hazy.

Too late, too late, I am already dead.

I was dead the moment I left the island. I knew it really even as I left, and still I had to go. Isn't it good enough for me.

I can't get this skrake off me. It's annoying me now even if I am done for. I manoeuvre a knee up into its chest and I push and with the weight of it off me I gulp the air into me and reach for my dagger. The stink is all over me. I get my dagger to its throat and sink it into the skin. I cut and press while nails and teeth scrape and clench. The skrake is weakening. I cut harder, faster, till it stops. Its weight becomes slack, the teeth give up their gnashing, but I keep cutting, tearing through leathery muscle and tendons and then bone and gristle. The blood is everywhere, my own blood flowing hot and fast down my neck.

With a great heave I push the last of it, its dead legs and arm off me and lie on the ground. The sky is above me, just the same, rolling grey and white and wild. The sea shifts and whispers and looks inviting.

I roll shakily and get to my feet, facing the enemy, my dirty knife ready, but even as I do I cannot help looking again to the sea. It takes me a moment to find them, in the mist: they're far off, nearly out of sight. Nearly safe.

I want more skrake blood on me.

My legs are shaking beneath me and it's hard to take in what's happening. *Shock*, Maeve says. *Rest, with your legs a little above your head. Keep warm.* I can see what's happening but it's far away. There are people on the beach, dark figures. My eyes go to one of them, then another, and with a thud of my heart I let myself think for a moment it's Mam and Maeve, working towards me. It is them, it is. I blink again and they're gone and I let myself fall down as far as my knees. Cold water from the wet sand seeps up my legs. *This is death*, I think.

There are shapes on the ground, too. Skrake. Their bloody bodies make dark red patches on the beach. Some are still moving, but others are only a tangled mess, mixing with the rain into dirty pink puddles. My eyes, though, my eyes will not stop coming back to the pair fighting: the way they move together, there's something in it, something too familiar, something I know well for myself.

I drag an arm across my eyes, forgetting it is covered in blood. I'm afraid for a moment but then I remember, I've been bitten. It doesn't matter now. I blink through the rain and look around for something to put my knife through.

The figures on the beach come into better focus. There are more – women, I can see now, battling the skrake – ten, twelve of them, working in pairs like the first two. Familiar. I am dying and maybe this is what happens. *Hallucinations*, my mind mumbles.

All around me, women fight. I move through them – I must have stood up again, I don't remember. To my left, I see a skrake reaching for a woman, trying to hold on to her by her short hair. The knife in my hand jumps from it as if of its own accord and flies, hitting the skrake between the eyes. A perfect shot. It twitches and lets go, and the woman looks around wildly for whoever threw the knife, meets my eyes, nods, turns back to finish things.

Good, I think. Good.

I can't focus on anything, my eyes want to be every-where but the pain of being bit makes my eyes cloudy and unfocused. Even still, I can see the way the women move, fluid and perfect. One skrake is down and they're working on another, the one with my last knife in its head, one holding its arms while the other reaches for the throat.

There's a thud and a feeling of discomfort in my knees and nose, and the scene in front of me doesn't look quite right. I have fallen to my knees again, I realise a moment later. I watch everything and understand nothing.

All the skrake are on the ground now, and the women are picking their way through them. One has a weapon that looks like a walking stick but has a long, curved blade at the end of it. As I watch her she makes a practised movement with the blade and a twitching skrake at her feet lies still.

At last I can make sense of what I'm watching.

These are banshees.

They fight just like Maeve and Mam did.

They look just like me.

Chapter Thirty-Six

MAEVE CAME ALIVE THEM LAST FEW DAYS BEFORE SHE died.

'You're gone quiet, hah?' she says to me after a good half-day of ignoring my surliness. 'Good girl. Hide yourself.'

Already her voice sounds better, stronger.

I keep up my stony silence while we make camp and eat eggs and potatoes with seaweed and peas. I keep a half-eye on her while she watches the country around us as it darkens; her eyes are lit up, her movements quick and sure. It's nearly like going back in time, so it is. It's disorientating.

We stay mostly out of the rain, and in the late afternoon I see where she's bringing us to: a mostly fallen-down building in the sheltered side of a hill. It's hidden away, part of the land around it. The walls are intact enough to keep us well hidden, but there's clear air above us for a fire. Once it's dark nobody'd see the smoke.

Maeve bids me light one and I think about disobeying but I'm cold, as well she knows. We'd the dinner ate then, and I've not a word to say to her nor she to me till the next day so we turn into ourselves and look for sleep.

I wait a long time for it, listening to Maeve coughing, but then she's shaking me and it's light so I must've slept long and well. I slept better than I should have and I wonder, did Maeve keep watch? Had she any sleep herself?

'Let's go hunting,' she says to me, and she smiles.

We walk a little back the way we came, and then north-west till we get to a jagged, wooded place. Maeve knows well where to go. At a stream we fill our bottles and then, walking quietly on, Maeve stiffens and points to the ground. The markings are hard to see at first and then I recognise them everywhere: smudges and lines in the mud, leading through the cover ahead of us. I know already that it's hard to come across tracks, that the afternoon rain washes everything clear again, unless it's under cover. Even with Maeve knowing where to look we're lucky to find these.

'One kill,' Maeve tells me, her voice low, 'and we'll head for home. Come on.'

I'm silent and not because I'm getting her back for

all her silences, or because of Mam, or because she wouldn't let me go, even. I'm silent because my heart has pulsed up through my throat into my mouth and if I open it I think it'll fall right out and I'll die there on the damp ground of pure fright.

We come upon the skrake in a clearing. We're upwind and hidden well but Maeve is moving too fast to let me stop and catch my breath and prepare.

'Ready?'

I shake my head, eyes pleading with her.

'You're ready.' She brushes my hair back from my forehead so she can kiss me, and then throws herself into the clearing, yelling like a madwoman wielding her stick, her staff, like a weapon.

I know if I wait even an instant I won't be able to move, I'll be stuck, so I throw myself after her. I try to find my voice to scream.

I shriek, I burst from the cover, my hands to my knives, my feet flying. The skrake and Maeve are facing off but when it sees me it turns, just like Maeve said it would, and just as we practised she gets behind it. She's in close and has her staff up across its body so it's pinned against her. Its teeth snap, inches from Maeve's face. I never knew how brave she was till this moment, I never understood the pure guts she had, she and Mam.

I am frozen, staring and caught while it writhes and

screams for me, and Maeve hangs on dearly, shouting over the screams of the skrake for me to go for my knives. She cannot hang on for ever.

It's only once the monster is nearly away from her that I remember to attack but I'm flustered, my knife seems to stick and I drop it. Maeve is struggling and thoughtlessly, panicking, I run for the skrake and leap, wrapping my arms around it while Maeve gets out away.

Oh god, the smell, the rot, the feel of it under my fingers.

Maeve has the space now to do that thing I've seen her do a million times, a leap and spin in the air, all of her strength and speed bundled up into the end of her staff and it connects so solidly to the skrake's head that I feel it all the way into my toes. I leave go, step back. The skrake barely pauses but Maeve's already on it, her legs pinning its arms and I watch for what's needed but she's her knife in her hand and her hand skin-deep in the neck and the whole thing is over quicker than I could count to twelve or twenty maybe.

We're in a heap, breathing hard. Laughter bubbles up from nowhere and I let it out.

The second skrake we see coming from ages off, that same day on our way home. It's midday-ish and I'm feeling so cocky walking that road, my back straight and arms swinging and eyes flashing. Let them at me, I'm thinking.

251

It's good to see another skrake, to have another go before we're home again and I can take stock and think about the next thing.

The skrake is a dull shape and you'd know it by its movements more than anything else at this distance. The twitching and shambling. The speed of it, though. It shambles towards us, the third skrake I'd ever seen, awkward but fast, and Maeve tells me to get ready.

'I'm ready,' I tell her, and I smile at her and she nods back at me, her eyes smiling at me.

My heart climbs up into my mouth and takes residence there again, despite how full of myself I am, but Maeve is smooth and strong and easy beside me. We fall into our stances, protecting each other. Our knives fly. When it's time, though, it goes for me instead of Maeve. I get my hands up and Maeve is on it in a flash. Things happen the way they're supposed to and Maeve and I put it down together.

Maeve and I, we put it down together.

Of course the skrake gets up again.

Maeve is careless, just for a second, and for maybe the first time in her life. It's her cold, muddling her head. She rests close to the corpse, her hands on her knees and she's wheezing and bending forwards so she can stifle her cough with her forearm, even then, a movement that is about caring for me. The skrake jerks up and gets her, going in deep for her hip. Not so far from where Mam was got.

Before I can even yell Maeve has her knife hilt-deep in the skrake's skull and it's dead a third time.

I can't *believe* it. I don't believe it. Maeve won't die this way, now, in front of me, despite all my experience of what terrible things can happen so quickly.

Maeve knows better. She lifts up the layers of clothes to look but she already knows. The bite barely breaks the skin, it's a scratch. It doesn't matter.

'Make it quick, little warrior,' is all she says to me and then she grits her teeth and rides out the agony of turning.

I watch her, hugging my knees. Nothing happens in my head, not even fear; there's only a stale blankness, an aggressive whiteness of silence while Maeve writhes. I can't even get up to hold her hand.

After a while her screams die away and her eyes find mine and hers are full of fear. Something in her is gone and I never see it again. Her gaze moves away from mine and then her eyes go still and they half close. And then I'm watching two bodies on the ground and feeling a long way from home.

It happens so fast, violence like that, but the silence afterwards is always the same. Eventually the world starts to encroach again, I hear the wind, and birds, and feel stones underneath me. Nothing has changed in the world except everything, for ever.

Maeve, my whole family.

My whole world and the last person in it.

I try to imagine pushing my knife through her head. I think about dragging her body along the ground and away from the mess of skrake beside her. Her lovely hands limp, her strong legs useless, her head dragging against the ground because I cannot lift her right. I think about burying her body, badly because I've only my hands. I think about the dirt getting all over her hair, getting into her eyes and ears.

I imagine going home then, after I'd buried her, frightened and sobbing and *done*.

I imagine sitting in the house on my own with that silence around me.

For ever.

And I know I'd rather die than stay there on that manmade afterthought of land by my lonesome, loathsome self with nothing but the ghost of a dead world all around me and that's the truth of it.

Twelve days. That's how long it took Mam, and she came round at the end; she was like herself, nearly. She could talk, she listened to me. A little, at least.

And Maeve knows, I know she knows, where Phoenix City is.

She'll come around. And maybe if we're close, if we're off east, she can show me; maybe in her final madness she'll tell me how to find it. Maybe she'd even tell me where they came from, the two of them.

Maeve said it was different for everyone and she is strong but she'd no fight left. I'll hurry. And if we can't get there, or if we get there and it's gone, or if we don't get there and die on the road, each one of those things is better than going back to the island and living and dying alone.

I leave Maeve's body. I go back to the island and I try again to imagine staying there, and instead I get the barrow, the same barrow Maeve carried my dead mother in, I pack chickens into a crate and I say goodbye to the house. I head out towards hope. There's nothing for it now but what I can do with my feet and hands and head and heart.

Chapter Thirty-Seven

I WATCH THE BANSHEE WARRIORS FROM MY SITTING-PLACE on the beach with my mouth open.

From the left, someone touches my shoulder. Reflexively I move to grab the wrist that is attached to the hand that is on me. It's another banshee and I don't hear her, maybe because she moves so light or maybe because of the sea of noise and pain at the side of my head.

She says, 'All right?'

I think that's what she says.

She says, 'Hey!'

I watch her lips move and then go back to looking at a decapitated skrake on the sand before me. Everything feels far away, beyond reach. My legs are cold from the sea, my ear feels like it's on fire. My stomach gives a lurch and I wonder if I'm going to throw up.

The banshee has knelt beside me and is looking me over. 'You were bitten?'

I know she's speaking but still I can't take in what she is saying to me. She looks familiar nearly, and then I remember that this is the same banshee I helped with my throwing-knife during the battle, the one that nodded at me. So I nod back at her now and then turn my eyes back to the carnage.

The banshee calls and waves to another nearby, shouting, 'Ciara! We've a bite here!'

A moment and then a shout back to her. 'On my way, Agata.'

The women move through the horde like a knife through flesh. Banshees are scythes, neatly parting every thing from its own self.

'The fire. Did you light that?'

I don't think I could answer her even if I knew what to say. And besides – I keep forgetting – I'm bit. I don't have to worry about it any more. *At least I get this*, I think, *at least I get to see these people, these banshees. At least I know what they were and what I am.*

I knew it, a little, already.

I expect Maeve to have some retort for me but she's only silence.

Another one of the banshees moves towards us. I watch

her mostly because I don't even have to move my head to do so. I have no energy, no answer for anything. She wears black like the others. Her wrists, from her hands right up to her elbows, are bandaged and bulky-looking. She has things on her ankles, and her hair is cut short – all of them have short hair, short like mine and Maeve's and Mam's. That's not it, though, the only reason I know we're the same, even though we look different; our skin colours and the shapes of our bodies and our faces. It's in the movement: light and strong and confident, and the way they fight. The way I was trained to fight.

There is something wrong with the balance of this new banshee's head, with the symmetry of it. She has moved out of my eye-line to crouch next to me with the other banshee before my mind can catch on this peeling edge of a thought.

The two banshees are talking with each other and I tune in, try to decipher their fast-moving tongues and low speech.

But now they are talking to me, trying to talk to me. The first one is telling me to do something, holding her hand in front of my face. I can't seem to focus on what she's saying, my eyes wander off towards the bloody battlefield again.

She slaps me hard in the face. The sting is nothing to the ache already in my head but the shock brings tears to my eyes. I take a deep shuddering breath and the world narrows for a moment.

'Here,' says the banshee, and against the hardness of her hand her voice is soft and gentle. The right side of my face is hot; it matches the left side, warmed from the blood from the bite. It feels like a blush, like shame. I breathe out, a vocal kind of sigh, and the noise I make sounds very small against all the noise of the carnage.

'Keep your head still, look at my hand,' the banshee Agata says again, and I try to do as she says, to look at her hand. If she hits me again I think I might cry and I don't want to cry now, when I'm so close to the end. Not in front of the banshees.

'What's your name, honey? Ciara, help her.'

'Still with us?' Ciara asks.

Agata reaches for something on her hip and the movement is familiar to me. It is like my own, or Maeve's. I pitch away but am steadied by strong, sure hands.

'Hold her.'

Ciara contorts herself to pin my arms, while Agata holds my head, pointing the wounded part upwards. I do not struggle hard but I can feel her strength against mine. She has a knife.

My eyes have lost the run of themselves entirely now. They're only interested in what's going on behind her, on the battlefield. They want to take in all they can before my death, which seems imminent. All this running – twice I've run that road – and death was here for me all along on this lonely beach, with home nearly in view. There are more banshees, picking through the bloody wreckage of the road in the mist. They all wear black. They too have short hair and the same bulky-looking forearms wrapped in black cloth to the elbow. They are tall and small, wide and slim, dark and pale, lithe and powerful.

The woman with the knife has grabbed on to the remains of my ear and she saws viciously at it. The pain, the sudden, sour ache of it makes me shout. My vision blurs. I feel nausea, I feel a letting go. This is the end, the end at last.

Nearly worse than the agony is the gristly sound it makes. Agata's blade scratches and tears, hewing through the cartilage in three long movements, and I scream as hard and loud as I can.

'Good girl, go easy now, don't faint on us,' the one holding my head says, and the other, nearly finished her work, answers: 'Yeah, we're too tired to be carrying you.'

Ciara laughs. I blink, and tears and snot run down my face.

'All done. Have you anything clean?'

Someone takes my hand and puts a cloth in it, and then brings my hand to where my ear used to be, the gaping wound on the side of my face, and presses it hard against my skull.

'Hold it there now,' she advises. 'Hold it tight so the bleeding will stop.'

My arms feel weak but I do what she says. Does this mean I might survive the bite? I put the thought away for later.

One of them moves off to join the others poking around in the pile of dead skrake on the ground. As I watch, a roar of thunder bellows around us, and the rain, already torrential, sets to with new determination.

There's an arm around me, a hand under an armpit and then another at my waist, forcing me upwards.

'You're all right, good girl. Come on with us.' I can barely hear them but I know the encouraging noises they're making.

She takes her hands up off me slowly, as if seeing whether I'll be able to stand on my own two feet and when I don't fall, she moves on a little ahead, looking back often to make sure I'm keeping up. I'm moving, my mind a blank. Something in the battlefield catches my eye and I stop suddenly.

The banshee glances back. 'Come on,' she says, and reaches a hand towards me.

I turn away from her, find the skrake that I killed, the one that has bits of my ear in its mouth and down its throat: I crouch to put my knee on its throat and a little awkwardly I pull my knife from its skull. It comes away cleanly and I go to wipe it on my damp, filthy skirt but my hands are shaking too much so in the end I put it back, dirty, to its place, hidden at my ankle. The banshee is looking at me: I cannot read the expression on her face.

'All right?'

I don't answer.

'I'm Agata,' she says. 'I'll be your shadow.'

I don't understand anything she's saying, I can't hear properly anyway. One ear is ringing and the other is gone gone gone and sounds only like heat and pain and the waves on the beach back home.

She takes two steps closer and I back away a little but she's smiling and her eyes are soft. She reaches out, slow so as not to frighten me, and touches my cheek.

'You'll be OK,' Agata says, so loudly and clearly that it reaches me. My eyes fill with fresh tears. She makes me lift the rag away from the wound at the side of my head, looks at it, then pushes my hand back again, showing me that I should keep more pressure on it. 'Don't let anyone else see that knife, OK? They'll only take it off you.' When she turns to walk away again I follow her without thinking.

Shaking with tiredness and cold and shock, I stumble and slip my way through sludge of the corpses in the road back towards the village in a daze.

Agata walks a little ahead. It's easier if I just let my feet follow her feet and don't look around too much. I do not like the feeling of a person being so close, but I'm grateful she says nothing when I stop suddenly at the side of the road to vomit up something sticky and yellow, half-digested shtorella.

I stay like that, leaning over with my hands on my bent legs, swaying a little in the cold and dark. When I'm pretty sure I won't be sick again, I wipe my mouth with the back of one bloody, trembling hand and look up to find her again but she's striding off across the battlefield. Battle-beach.

Dazedly I watch as she looks about her, goes a little further, then kneels to pull something from a corpse. The movement is familiar: she is gathering her knife back to her. I blink and look away and then I see him.

Cillian.

He moves towards me, slipping in the gore, filthy hands outstretched, trying to balance, and then reaching for me. I go to him and when he wraps his arms around me I feel the world right itself a little, as if I'm tethered to it again, as if it has something to do with me after all.

'They're away?' he speaks quietly, so close to my good ear, my remaining ear, that I can hear him OK and I nod, my chin digging into his chest.

'Gone, through the mist.'

I feel him sag against me, the relief pouring out of him. He must've run so hard, following the banshees to get to the beach, terrified of what he'd find here.

'Say nothing to these.'

'Are you all right?' I ask.

'They got to me too soon. They came just before the skra—'

I'm only half-worrying about this sentence when there's a *whumph*, a shock I feel all through me like a hit, and Cillian goes limp in my arms. Behind him is Agata in her guard and I see then what has happened. She hit him so hard I could feel it right through him and he is *out*. I let him fall, gently, to the beach.

Agata towers over him, knife in hand, and without thinking I put myself between them. 'Don't!' I say, looking right at her, seeking out her eyes, finding them. 'Please don't.' There's a beat while Agata hesitates, balancing on the balls of her feet, and then her eyes flick around us. Nobody is watching. 'Please!' I shout, hoping someone will look over, put a stop to it.

'He's an enemy of the city,' Agata says. 'He tried to get away.'

'Please, Agata, please.' My voice is unrecognisable, yelping.

'He'd be better off,' she says quietly.

'Please,' I say again. 'Hasn't it been enough?'

I don't know if what I'm saying makes sense to her at all, but she lowers her hand and falls out of guard, and at last, at last, the battle is over.

Chapter Thirty-Eight

THEY'VE A BIG SQUARE OF TOUGH PLASTIC WITH TWO loops of rope at the front and they put Cillian on the plastic and then two banshees each take a loop and they drag him along after them. I follow on. They do it easily; the banshees take turns, working to some invisible schedule they all know of.

I watch Cillian and Agata watches me.

It is dark. The rains are past now and the cold is settling down but it doesn't slow them. The pain I have, the vicious shout of it to the side of my head makes my knees weak and my stomach gurgle. It's all I can do to keep up with them.

They move with a purpose. I try not to think, only walk at the back of the group, keeping my eyes on Cillian's face, his blank expression and soaked hair.

The banshees make camp a little off to the north of the big road that leads back to Phoenix City. I could not say how long it takes to get there. I'm so tired I'm dropping. There's a fire with a small blue flame giving heat and I am put in front of it and given water and then some food, which I cannot eat. I draw my knees up to my chin and wrap my arms around my legs. I close my eyes in the warmth.

When I wake it's light and the camp is empty except for all their gear. A blanket has been put over me, woolly on one side and plastic on the other, and the fire is still going; I'm warm, I'm mostly dry. Gingerly I touch the side of my face and then Agata is at my side. She has brought me water and I drink some. Next she takes my unresisting hands in hers and ties them together tightly.

'Just in case,' she tells me. 'Probably you're grand but a bite is a bite, hah?'

She holds my head carefully, tipping it one side tenderly and it feels good, it feels nice to be touched softly like that, till she fingers the wound. I flinch.

'Go easy,' she says, and it's so good to have someone there, to have a person who'll tell me what the best thing is to do. 'Hurts like a shitter and the next few days you won't feel great. Probably you'll be grand after that.' She daubs something on me and the flesh stings and then gets warmer and begins to itch.

'Where's Cillian?'

She nods her chin towards one of the little ruins of stone buildings, but doesn't stop what she's doing. I drink her in now I've a chance to see her in the full light of day, while her eyes are busy elsewhere. Her skin is a deep brown, so unblemished it nearly looks like it's moist.

I imagine Cillian, his slight, pale body curled over, his arms drawn up to his face. I wonder how cold he was last night while I slept comfortable near the fire.

'Is he OK?' I ask.

'You don't know that guy, OK?' She's taken my jaw and pointed it towards her so we're staring straight at each other. It's uncomfortable, we're so close, and I try to ease back but she doesn't let me, she holds on tight. Her voice is low and urgent. 'If anyone asks do you know what happened to the women he was with, you don't know that either.' She keeps working on her knife though it's shining already. 'You understand me?'

I glance towards the ruins.

'Blink if you do,' she says, and I blink, nearly accidentally.

'Walk with me today, steer clear of him.'

'Where are the others?'

'Morning exercises.'

'Not you?'

'I've to guard you,' she says, pulling gently on the rope binding my hands together.

The other banshees are heading back our way. I can hear their voices, the sounds of human feet moving through shrubs and trees.

'And Cillian?'

'You don't know him, you don't know his name.' She's speaking quickly, getting the words out before the rest of them get back to the camp. She sighs, glances over her shoulder. 'He'll come with us.'

'What will happen him?' I ask, but the other banshees are moving around the fire, talking loudly, joking, and Agata says no more.

I sit back. I watch them. This will be my role, my strategy: to watch quietly, to listen, to do what I am told. I can be safe now that I have what I want: to have people, to be on the way to the city.

I can do nothing for Cillian with Agata watching me. I could do nothing for him anyway.

The banshees and Cillian and me, we move east towards the city. My third time walking this hungry road.

We move so fast. My legs can keep up but my thinking is overrun. It is too much for me, the losses, my wounds, the banshees' great, confident presence, walking the road as if they've every right to be there. The load of them moving in pairs, all except Agata who stays with me. They talk, they sing, they light their small, blue fires. They kill whatever they happen across, which is mostly skrake. They take joy in it.

Quiet your whisht, girl, only listen, Maeve tells me, and I do, I stay quiet.

Cillian is quiet, too. I see him when the banshees are packing up. We don't look at each other, and I can feel Agata watching me. I go with her to the top of the walking column that the banshees make and he stays towards the back of it. I've seen enough, though. They've his feet tied as well as his hands. I see the way he has crumpled under the weight of whatever it is that'll happen to him in Phoenix City. To these banshees he is nothing.

We move, the banshees walking ahead and behind of me as if they belong here. As if this world is theirs.

I work hard to keep up. My mother was a banshee and I've been trained as a banshee and I can walk any road as fast as them, with a hole in the side of my head or not. This is it, I keep thinking.

Before we moved out there were a lot of questions about where I came from and how long I've been out here. I don't know how to answer them; I stay on being quiet. To put words together is to make sense of a thing, and I've no shapes to put to the world around me. The banshees make a point of shoving me around and the one they all look to, Mare, loses her patience. She hits a belter, and she doesn't shy off from the injured side of my head. I feel the pain all the way to my toes, all the way into my bones. She hits like a rock – it's like being hit by Maeve nearly – and the place where my ear used to be rings all day after it.

'Don't take it personally,' Agata tells me quietly, later, and I nod a little to show her I understand. I do as well. They must know I know something about their runaways. They stare at me a lot, there's an anger coming off them, but nobody hits me again. The banshees – Ciara, Lin, Anna, Sene, Niamh, more as well; I listen thirstily for their names – they talk a lot, quiet between themselves but nearly constant. It's hard to understand their accents and anyway, when I get snatches it's only about people I don't know or things that happened I don't have any knowledge of, about people in the city, about other banshees. They train: stretches and exercises in the morning. Press-ups, the last few on the knuckles. There'll be sparring in the evening.

It's the way they move through the land I like about them, it's that I can't stop watching. It's *unapologetic*. The hunger they have for the country around us is familiar to me. We'll stop to rest and drink water and a pair of them will leave the group to climb a hill or investigate a building or go chasing after tracks I never noticed on the ground. The way they walk is casual and easy and full of power. I want to get a bit of that.

I mourn Maeve in those long silences on the road when the banshees are quiet. I try to imagine Nic and Aodh rowing west through the mist while we move east. Finding home, the two of them, together, safe. In my head, though, they keep transforming into Mam, pregnant with me, and Maeve, loving her, and the two of them safe and happy with years ahead of them still.

In the quiet in my own head, the roaring silence heals over and I begin to think again. I watch the banshees closely and, with hands left untied now, I move a bit more like them. I practise it. I practise being bold on the road. I pretend that I am powerful too.

It is night. If I don't do it now there won't be much point in doing it, and I've to do it so. There it is.

I asked for water after dinner which was a small bit of a salty, crumbly hard thing and a few bites off one of the rabbits Sene had killed in the morning. I kept the canten after Agata gave it to me, hid it under my bit of blanket so she wouldn't think of it, and she didn't.

They're asleep now, except for the one on watch, and she's nodding even as she stands, facing away from me at the other side of the fire. I watched where they'd put Cillian and he's on his own, tied up under a shelter fifty paces off. It's cruel, so it is, not to let him have the heat of the fire at night.

I move as if it's all going to go OK, with confidence and speed and silence. Like one of them. The banshees sleep close around the fire, some of them curled up against each other. There's the noise of breathing and scratching and a half-snore from Mare. There was coming and going as people go off into the bushes to shit after dinner, but not now. Now it's quiet and everyone, nearly everyone, is properly out.

Now is good. Now is the time.

As I'm moving away from the campfire the one on duty shifts in her stance and I freeze against the blackness before moving again, not straight out to where Cillian is tied up but backwards, further into the gloom so that if she turns the whole way around she wouldn't see me. She won't miss my body in the mess of the group on the ground, I'd say.

I'm away, and though I can still see not so much the fire as the soft blue glaze it puts on the things around it, the blankets and bodies of the banshees and the rocks, they won't see me, not from here.

They have him tied in such a way that it's hard to lie down and he's sitting instead with his back against a crumbling concrete wall. He's asleep, as asleep as he can be; he can't put his arms around himself, they're tied too tight, but he has tried. The first thing I do is put my blanket over him and when I do his eyes open. I put my hand over his mouth till he's more awake, till I know he sees me properly.

Looking into his eyes I feel nearly giddy.

He's alive, I'm alive.

'Hi,' I say, and I take away the palm of my hand from his lips.

His lip is swollen, and when he opens his mouth to talk his voice is slurred. Of course they'd questions for him as well.

'What are you doing here?'

I shush him, then whisper, 'Setting you free.'

He's silent, shivering into the blanket, while I reach for the knife with the golden handle, my mam's knife, strapped in its place at my ankle. It doesn't take long to get through the ropes but it takes ages to get him to be able to stand, he's so stiff with hurt and cold.

'Will you be all right?'

He doesn't answer for a long moment and I wonder again am I doing the right thing.

'I'm OK,' he says. I don't believe him.

'Come on,' I say, and we walk a little along the road together, further away from the banshees. He begins to stand straighter, to move quicker. He'll be OK.

'Do you know where you are?'

He looks up and down the road in the black night.

'It's the same road,' I say, 'just keep going that way. You remember how to get there, how to find the beach again?'

There'll be no boat for him: he'll have to find a way, to manage somehow.

Cillian doesn't answer for a long time and I want to shake him.

'You're not coming?' he says.

I've no answer for him that he doesn't know already.

'Here, you've water, and a blanket. If you start now, you've half a night's start. You'll make it.'

'Why aren't you coming? They'll know it was you. They won't believe I got away on my own.'

He's right I'd say.

'Here,' I say, and I hand him, hilt-first, my mother's knife. 'Now you've a knife as well.'

'Orpen, I don't know how to—'

'It belongs on the island,' I tell him. 'Hold on to it for me there.'

He's more awake now, he's alert. He pushes the blanket back at me. 'If this is gone they'll know for sure it was you. I'll be all right.'

I don't take it but he thrusts it at me, and then the water as well.

'OK,' I say.

He doesn't move, only stays staring at me.

'Go, Cillian,' I tell him.

'I wish you'd come with me.'

There's another silence.

'Cillian—'

I'm glancing back towards the camp when he does it,

taking my face in his hands and putting his swollen mouth to mine. His fingers hold my battered face so tenderly, so carefully, I could cry. He kisses me. It's done and finished before I know what's happening even.

I think about it for the whole rest of life.

'Thank you,' he says, and then he's gone, shuffling into the night, holding my knife, Mam's knife, and nothing else.

I steal back to where he was kept, feeling along the road till I have what I want, and then I kneel down where his frayed ropes are on the ground. I take the sharp stone I found and put it down next to them.

I come back round the fire again, back towards where my sleeping-place is, the canten slung on my shoulder, the blanket that Cillian wouldn't take around my shoulders. I go quiet and slow and I adjust my front in case anyone's looking so it'll look like I'm only back from a piss.

I settle down in the cosy warmth of the fire and I look about and I could nearly smile, cuddling up again underneath my blanket.

My eyes meet Agata's.

Hers are wide open, staring at me, speculative and unblinking.

We wake before the dawn and rise together, all of us.

After I turned from Agata and lay down again, I waited. It wasn't till the change of the watch Cillian was missed.

There is talk of going after him but it's subdued. The banshees are tired, but a handful of them go off jogging into the night to see can they find him. I lie very still, as if I am not there, not daring to so much as breathe in Agata's direction. She stays quiet, too. After a long time I fall back to sleep.

When the banshees get up, I get up, and when they go off for morning exercises together I don't stay beside the heat of the fire. I am my mother's daughter. I am Maeve's as well.

Agata shadows me and when the banshees begin to go through their exercises, I keep after them. We get into the push-ups and the banshees, they watch me out of the corners of their eyes. I work hard, though I'm stiff and out of condition, till their eyes move on.

'Will we spar this evening?' I ask Agata. I'm loosened up, I'm ready for it. I want to see what she's like, and what I'm like now.

We pack up the camp then and on we go, on towards the city. We move once more through the bloodied road under angry skies.

Acknowledgements

Thanks to Dave Rudden and conferences.

Thanks to Lisa Coen. I am so lucky to be hanging around you.

Thanks to friends who have had to listen to me bang on about this for literally years: Bex Coghlan, Lou Hodgson (who read things first), Susie Hill, Hannah Murphy, Marco Herbst.

Thanks to Sallyanne Sweeney and the gang at Mulcahy Associates, there's nowhere I'd rather be.

Thanks to the incredible Mary-Anne Harrington who really inspires me as a publisher, to Amy Perkins, and to everyone at Tinder Press and Headline.

Thanks to Georgina Moore who is a force of nature, and thanks to the brilliant Elaine Egan.

Huge thanks too to Christine Kopprasch and the team at Flatiron, I feel really proud to be published by you in the US.

Thanks to the exceptional readers of Ireland – there's no place like home, especially for books.

Thanks to my brothers, Will Danger, Hens, and James.

Thanks most of all to my parents, Robert and Sheelagh.

Sarah Davis-Goff's writing has been published in the *Irish Times*, the *Guardian* and LitHub. This is her first novel. She was born and lives in Dublin.